THE **CURSE** ᴏꜰ
JONATHAN MATTHEW

THE CURSE OF
JONATHAN MATTHEW

JOHN F. GREEN

Stoddart

*Stoddart Publishing gratefully acknowledges the support of the
Canada Council and the Ontario Arts Council in the development
of writing and publishing in Canada.*

Published in 1997 by
Stoddart Publishing Co. Limited
34 Lesmill Road
Toronto, Canada M3B 2T6
Phone: (416) 445-3333
Fax: (416) 445-5967
e-mail Customer.Service@ccmailgw.genpub.com

Distributed in the United States by
General Distribution Services Inc.
Toll free 1-800-805-1083
e-mail gdsinc@genpub.com

Cataloguing in Publication Data

Green, John F., (John Frederick), 1943–
The curse of Jonathan Matthew

ISBN: 0-7736-7455-1

I. Title.

PS8563.R416C87 1997   jC813'.54   96-990076-7
PZ7.G73Cu 1997

Cover design: Tannice Goddard
Cover art: Sharif Tarabay
Computer Graphics: Mary Bowness

Printed and bound in Canada

*This story is for Jim and Edna Bell who live on
Glebe Road in Warlingham . . .*

with affection and thanks.

THE DREAM

Werylingham, Surrey, 1194

The villagers whispered about it in the square, in the shops, in the saddlery and the blacksmith. They whispered in the tithing office and the market. About the baker's boy, Jonathan Matthew, and about Baker's Hill Road where they found the ax.

They whispered about it in the church where they had placed Jonathan's body, and where his blood stained the altar.

Poor Jonathan, snatched away before preparations could be made.

No body. No burial.

The soldiers whispered about what they'd seen on the road to the village, and what was in the pond.

They all whispered about the royal visitor.

With their eyes shifting and cautious, heads barely apart, the villagers whispered back and forth.

Whispered about Jonathan Matthew.

Whispered.

Especially about the curse.

CHAPTER ONE

Veronica Shaw's spoked wheels cut through trails of mist rising from a roadway damp with morning dew. At seven in the morning, shops were still closed, their windows staring blankly over the steaming deserted sidewalks — the prelude to a hot and muggy July day.

As she leaned into the Hill Street corner, Veronica urged the bike into high gear, taking the turn wide, narrowly missing a garbage truck creeping along the curb.

"Watch where you're going!" an angry

voice shouted after her. "Stupid kid!"

The insult went ignored. Veronica's single-minded mission—to get to Benjamin Hilton's house—kept her legs pumping and her eyes straight ahead.

As the rear of the Hilton house came into view she braked, jerking the ten-speed onto the driveway, and coming to a sliding stop at the back gate.

The first few weeks of summer heat had turned the Hilton back yard into an explosion of color. Peonies lined the flagstone walk and the lattice surrounding the porch was drenched with purple and white clematis.

But Veronica's thoughts were far from the beauty of flower gardens. She was bursting with incredible news and she was going to die if she didn't tell someone in the next thirty seconds.

Her insistent finger on the doorbell finally brought Mrs. Hilton scurrying to the door in her bathrobe.

"Veronica! What on earth—"

"Hi, Mrs. Hilton, I mean good morning. Is Benjamin here?"

"Of course, but he's still in bed. Is something wrong?"

"Can you get him up? This is really important."

"Well, yes, I suppose so, but—"

"That's okay, I'll do it." Veronica was across the kitchen floor in a flurry of arms and legs before Mrs. Hilton had a chance to protest.

"Wait, he might be—!"

"Don't worry," called Veronica, taking the stairs three at a time, "I'll keep my eyes shut."

The lump under the covers was curled into a ball with a pillow over its head. Veronica vaulted onto the footboard, balancing on one running shoe while prodding the lump with the other.

"Ben! Hey, Benjamin! Wake up! Wait till you hear the news!"

Slowly, Benjamin Hilton stretched, yawned, rolled over. An eye appeared, squinting at the shape looming at the end of the bed.

"Ben," Veronica started again, "you've got to hear this."

"Veronica Shaw," muttered a sleepy voice, "why are you standing on my bed?"

"Listen, Ben, you can't imagine what's happened—"

"GET OFF MY BED!" yelled Ben, clutching the sheets around him. "MOM, GET THIS MORON OFF MY BED!"

"Okay," Veronica shrugged, jumping to the floor. "Don't have a coronary. If you're not interested, that's fine with me. It just happens to be the greatest news since the invention of the double cheeseburger."

"It can at least wait till I'm dressed. Now get out of here."

Downstairs, Veronica slumped heavily into a kitchen chair. Her green eyes flashed as she flipped a mop of red hair away from her forehead.

"What do I get when I arrive with the greatest news since the four-slice toaster? I get called a moron!"

"Have some cereal," chuckled Mrs. Hilton. "Ben isn't the most amiable person in the world when he first wakes up."

By the time Ben stumbled into the kitchen

and plunked himself down, Veronica was pouring milk over her second bowl of corn flakes. She scowled at him. "You in a better mood now?"

"I'm not used to waking up at seven in the morning to find people standing on the end of my bed. What's so important it couldn't wait five minutes?"

Veronica's eyes came alive. "This morning my mother told me about a new contract her architectural company's signed."

"So?"

"It's in England, Ben. In England!"

Ben stopped spreading jam on his toast. "That's why you jumped on my bed?"

"You don't understand." The words began to tumble out. "There's an old church where the wall's falling down with an ancient curse and a ghost that walks around that needs to be fixed—the wall I mean—and she's going for the whole summer to live in a house and you and I and Eddy Miller are going with her."

There was a moment of stunned silence. Ben stared at Veronica, then turned to his mother.

"Your father and I were going to tell you about it tonight at dinner," Mrs. Hilton said, grinning broadly. "A sort of surprise, I guess."

It was Veronica's turn to stare. "You mean you know?"

"Of course. Your mother and Mr. Hilton and I have been discussing it for some time. There are still a lot of details that need working out. Your mother and the Millers are coming over this evening to discuss them."

"The three of us?!" breathed Ben. "That's awesome!"

"We're leaving as soon as passports can be arranged," added Veronica.

Ben was suddenly on his feet. "Eddy will flip when he hears this! Let's wake him up."

Before Mrs. Hilton could get a word out, Ben and Veronica were through the back door and across the porch.

"Actually," said Veronica as they steered their bikes down the driveway, "I'm a little worried about Eddie's reaction."

"Why?"

"I don't think he'll go for it. You know what he's like when it comes to the unknown."

"No problem," said Ben confidently. "I can read old Eddy like a book. He'll think it's a great idea."

* * *

"Are you two out of your minds?!" gasped Eddy Miller when he heard the news. "That's a foreign country, for crying out loud!"

"That's the whole idea," said Ben.

"I told you he'd freak," put in Veronica.

"Besides," Eddy continued, clutching his pajama tops, "my mother will never let me go."

"That's all been looked after," said Ben. "Our parents have been plotting behind our backs."

Edwin Bryson Miller sat on the edge of his bed staring at the grinning faces of the friends with whom he shared all his hopes and dreams and secrets—the only two friends he had in the world. His nervous nature put him at the mercy of every kid in grade five who dangled a spider in his face or jumped at him from around a corner. By the time each Friday rolled around,

Eddy was a wreck. It took him all weekend to recover.

Ben and Veronica hated the way the other kids treated Eddy, and so they never mentioned his nervousness.

At this moment, Eddy was doing his best to put up a brave front. "England!" he snorted loudly. "Just how do you plan on getting there?"

Veronica's eyes rolled upwards. "Ben and I are going to swim. I don't know about you."

"Don't be smart! You know what I'm talking about. I hate those jumbo jets."

"You've never been on one," said Ben.

"What's that got to do with anything?"

"Eddy," Veronica began patiently, "this is a great opportunity. Who knows what kind of adventures we might have? You'd regret it the rest of your life if you missed it."

"Famous last words!"

"Nobody's trying to con you, Eddy. Think of it—you can go somewhere you've never been before, learn something, and have fun, all at the same time. It's the chance of a lifetime."

Eddy looked at his two friends in disgust. "I can't think on a nervous stomach. I need some breakfast."

That much from Eddy was a definite maybe. Ben knew it was all he and Veronica were going to get.

* * *

Around the Hilton dinner table that evening there hovered an unusual air of anticipation. Ben's older sister Alison sensed something was going on, and she hoped it involved her brother. Especially if he was in some kind of trouble.

"I know what's up!" she burst out suddenly. "You and that Nervous Nellie Edwin Miller got caught pushing over mailboxes again."

"Moron," scowled Ben.

"This time you're going to jail," she said gleefully.

"Alison," scolded Mr. Hilton, "you have no idea what you're talking about. Marion Shaw and the Millers are coming over after dinner to discuss Ben's trip to England."

"Is that all?" said Alison, falling silent.

At eight o'clock, the Hilton doorbell chimed and Ben's mother welcomed the Millers, Veronica and Marion Shaw into the front hall. After all the 'hellos' and comments ("My, how the children are growing," and "It looks like we're in for a storm," and so on) were over, Mrs. Hilton served coffee and cake.

Ben, Veronica and Eddy sat quietly on the couch waiting for everyone to get comfortable. Finally, Mr. Hilton settled back in his chair. He eyed the three children mischievously.

"It seems the cat's already out of the bag and we've been upstaged."

"My fault, I'm afraid," said Marion Shaw. "I let it slip this morning at breakfast. And Miss NBC News here," she nodded at Veronica, "got away before I could stop her."

"All the more mysterious," said Eddy's father. "It's time to fill them in on the details."

"Well," Mrs. Shaw began, "as you know, the architectural firm I work for has a worldwide reputation for its specialty restoration work. And we've been contracted by the

Preservation of Ancient Buildings Society in Warlingham, a village in the county of Surrey. The foundation beneath the north wall of the old village church has given way. I've been assigned to the rebuilding project, which means I'll have to go there for the summer to supervise the work."

"And the church is haunted," Veronica jumped in, "with an ancient curse and everything."

"Yes," said Mr. Miller. "I read that in the newspaper. You know, Marion, the article they ran about your assignment—it made quite a thing about the legendary curse that surrounds the ancient church. Something about royalty and a lost treasure. Makes for good reading, I suppose."

Mrs. Shaw smiled. "There is a story about a curse, and a ghost that's been seen in and around the village, apparently only at a particular time of the year . . . rather odd. Mrs. Bell, the woman from the Society who's looking after our accommodations, mentioned it in one of her letters. During my interview for the paper, I made a reference to it, and the reporter must have phoned Mrs. Bell. The church is over eight hundred years old and, as you say, it's the kind of stuff people love to read."

"The English take their ghosts very seriously," Mrs. Hilton added.

Eddy's mother leaned towards the children suddenly. "Allowing you three to go to England with Mrs. Shaw was not an easy decision for any of us. We discussed it very carefully. England is very far away, and . . ."

"But," interrupted Marion Shaw, "since the Building Society has provided me with a house only a couple of streets from where I'll be working . . ." She turned to Ben's mother. "And since the Hiltons were kind enough to let Veronica spend her entire summer vacation last year with them at their cottage . . ."

"And," Ben's mother added sternly, "since we all know you three are sensible children, quite capable of looking after yourselves . . ."

"We've decided," concluded Mr. Hilton, "to give you the opportunity to accompany

Mrs. Shaw for the summer—that is, if you want to."

"Want to!" said Ben excitedly. "Of course we want to."

Veronica was on her feet. "How could we possibly say no?"

There was a quiet moment while everyone looked at Eddy.

"Eddy?" his mother asked finally.

"Well," said Eddy slowly, "I suppose someone will have to go with these two, to keep them out of trouble."

Mr. Hilton turned to Veronica's mother, "Then it's settled. It looks like they're yours for the summer."

"Fine," said Marion Shaw. "As soon as the passports are ready, we'll be on our way. It should be a grand summer."

* * *

Outside the Hilton house, the shadowy figure that had been hiding in the cedar shrubbery beneath the windows slipped into the sultry darkness that waited for the summer storm.

From his hiding place at the end of the

street, he'd watched the group make their way, laughing and talking, up the Hilton driveway and into the house. He'd recognized the architect from her picture in the paper, the one who was going to England, the one who would find the priceless treasure he sought so desperately. Once he spotted her, he didn't pay any attention to the others. They weren't important.

He'd waited while dusk descended over the street and lights winked on in the Hilton living room. When he was sure no one would see him, he slipped into the yard. Crouching as close as he could to the open window, he gathered every word, every scrap of information, into his greedy ears. He heard all the talk about the haunted churchyard, the ancient curse—and the royal treasure!

Then before they had time to say good-bye, he was gone.

CHAPTER TWO

For two weeks, the three friends lived in keen anticipation of their trip to Britain. They went on expeditions to the public library, looking for information about the history and people of Surrey. There was plenty to choose from—picture books, videotapes, travel brochures and tourist guides. But they found nothing about a curse, or a treasure at the church in the village of Warlingham.

"Well, it's too late to worry about it now," said Eddy, slamming shut a heavy encyclopedia. "We leave tomorrow, and I haven't even decided how many pairs of socks I'm taking."

Ben and Veronica exchanged glances. They knew that Eddy's socks would be the least of his worries.

* * *

The next morning, Toronto International Airport was jammed. Ben and Eddy hugged their parents one last time then, with Marion Shaw and Veronica, jostled and pushed their way slowly through the mob to the check-in counter.

Eddy started to complain. He was convinced the flight over the Atlantic was doomed. "What happens if we run out of fuel? There's a fuel shortage, you know."

"Don't worry," Veronica assured him, "they check those things very carefully."

"But what if the engines quit? We'll drop like a sack of bricks."

"That's ridiculous," said Ben, shaking his head.

"Airplane engines quit all the time," insisted Eddy.

Ben was getting annoyed. "There are four

engines. There is no way all four are going to quit at once."

"And what about—"

"Eddy!" Veronica poked him. "Cut it out!"

"Okay. All right. I just want you to know that I'm not entirely happy with this idea."

By the time they'd cleared security and were seated in the departure lounge, there was less than half an hour left before takeoff. Eddy was a nervous wreck.

"You can stop this anytime, Eddy," said Ben, when his friend continued to moan and carry on. "Thousands of people fly all over the world every day and get to where they're going in one piece."

"It's not them I'm worried about," Eddy mumbled. He was biting his nails yet again when the lounge speaker announced their flight.

"That's us," said Mrs. Shaw, stuffing her magazine away. "Everybody ready?"

It was a long walk along the ramp to the plane. Eddy made no attempt to hide his jitters. But once they were seated in the jet's wide and comfortable interior, he seemed to relax a little. During takeoff, with his eyes shut tight, he locked Veronica's arm in a death grip.

"You can let go now," she grimaced, prying his fingers loose. "We're on our way."

Finally, after Eddy had inspected his seat belt three times, checked to see that his window was securely fastened into the airplane, and asked the stewardess to make sure they had enough fuel, he fell asleep. Ben knew they wouldn't hear from him again.

An hour before they were due to land, Marion Shaw woke up, stretched and, with her overnight bag, headed for the rear of the plane. She had taken only a few steps when a tall man suddenly rose into the aisle and collided with her. The impact knocked her to her knees.

"Excuse me," the man muttered thickly, bending to help her. "Terribly clumsy. Do forgive me."

"It's quite all right." Mrs. Shaw straightened her jacket. "I probably wasn't watching where I was going."

The man's thin moustache twitched

nervously. "No, no, entirely my fault." He turned suddenly and continued down the aisle.

Veronica poked Ben. "Did you see that?"

"What?" Ben turned, just as the man passed their seat.

"That man. It looked like he bumped into my mother on purpose."

"What's wrong?" asked Eddy sleepily.

"Probably nothing," Veronica frowned. "Just looked odd, that's all."

The incident was soon forgotten in the preparations for landing. As the jet touched down, Eddy let out a great sigh of relief. Ben felt an electric thrill go through him. England! One of those places you read about in school or see in the movies, but never actually visit. But he was visiting. He was here with his two best friends, and they had an entire summer in front of them. He wanted to shout out loud with excitement.

"Now don't forget," warned Mrs. Shaw, "when we get into the terminal, we stick together."

Heathrow Airport was crowded with

people of every imaginable race and color. Between the customs desk and the outer lobby, Ben and Eddy heard eight different languages and counted a dozen ethnic costumes.

After passing several rows of boutiques, news-stands, and television monitors displaying flight information, they arrived at the luggage carousel. Twenty minutes later, their belongings piled around them, they settled onto a bench to collect their thoughts.

Marion Shaw searched her pockets. "My travel agent drew a map of the terminal, showing where to get bus information. Where have I put it?"

From the side pocket of her jacket, she produced two pieces of paper. One was covered in a network of lines and arrows, obviously the map she'd been looking for. The other was a tightly folded square of yellow newsprint that she almost pushed back without opening.

"What's that?" asked Veronica.

"Probably something left over from the office. Hold onto it for a moment while I sort out this map."

"Holy smoke!" her daughter exclaimed a moment later. "Look at this!"

On the faded page were two crudely written lines:

YOU VENTURE INTO THINGS UNNATURAL.
BEWARE!

"What on earth?!" cried Mrs. Shaw. She took the paper from Veronica and examined it carefully.

"Somebody is trying to tell you something," said Eddy uneasily, "and they're not being very subtle about it."

"But who? Why?"

"Mom!" Veronica's eyes lit up. "The man on the plane. The one who knocked you down."

"What about him?"

"He probably slipped the note into your pocket when he helped you up."

"That's silly! It was an accident. Besides, what possible reason could he have?"

"The curse," Eddy said ominously.

"Ridiculous!" snorted Mrs. Shaw.

"Do you think we should tell the police?" asked Ben.

"Of course not. It's nothing more than a silly practical joke. Let's forget the whole thing and find our bus."

As Veronica reached for her suitcase, her gaze fell on a set of exit doors across the lobby. Partially hidden behind them and watching their every move was the very man they'd been talking about.

"There he is!" she gasped. "The man on the plane."

The others turned. "Where?"

"There, by those exit doors," she pointed. "He's watching us."

For an instant, she took her eyes from the spot. When she looked again, the figure had disappeared into the crowd beyond the doors.

"You're giving me the creeps," said Eddy.

"You must have imagined it," said Marion Shaw, scanning the far side of the lobby. But the concerned expression on her face told another story, one she didn't seem comfortable with. "Come on, we have a bus to catch."

The bus ride from the airport to

Warlingham Village Green took the better part of four hours. The sun slowly burned its way through a heavy fog, until the day became quite warm.

The red double-decker pitched and rolled over narrow country roadways, plodding through one village after another. Each time it lurched around a corner, Eddy grabbed hold of anything within reach, convinced the bus was going to topple. They passed rows and rows of houses, all exactly alike, until Ben began to wonder if the journey would ever end.

Finally, after one more stretch of green hillside and one more village, the driver's Cockney accent announced Warlingham Green as the next stop. The tired group hopped off the high bus exit onto the curb in front of the White Lion Inn.

Before them was a large, triangular-shaped park, the center of the village. At one end, the road disappeared over a low hill. At the other, a bronze bust, green with age, kept vigil. Shops and narrow lanes lined both sides of the green.

Mrs. Shaw set her bag down. "We have to find the real estate office. Mrs. Bell will be waiting to show us our house."

"It's right over there," said Ben, indicating a small frame building down the street.

"Good," yawned Eddy. "I don't think I can stay awake much longer."

Mrs. Bell was a bright, cheery woman. "I'm on the Building Society Committee that hired you, Mrs. Shaw. We're all very anxious to meet you."

"Marion, please. And I'm looking forward to beginning the project. But right now I have three tired children to get settled. Is the house very far?"

"Right 'round the corner on Glebe Road." She removed a set of keys from the wallboard. "We'll be there in a jiffy."

The stone houses that lined Glebe Road were well-kept, most of them several centuries old.

"Your place is quite comfortable with lots of room," chatted Mrs. Bell. "It used to belong to the vicarage but became quite a financial burden. The Society took it over a few years ago to use as a guest residence."

They had almost reached the end of the street when Mrs. Bell pointed to a long driveway running between two houses. "Here we are. It's the Tudor place on the left."

The children and Mrs. Shaw stood before a narrow two-storey building with round stained glass windows set into the stone walls above the front door. It sat well forward on the lot, almost touching the street. The driveway ended at a pair of garage doors that looked as though they hadn't been opened in years.

"I'll not come in," said Mrs. Bell, handing over the key. "I know you're tired and anxious to get settled. You'll find everything's in place." A note of hesitancy crept into her voice. "I feel obliged to warn you, there are some here who don't share our enthusiasm for this venture."

"Oh, is something wrong?"

"Not wrong, exactly. More superstition than anything else."

"Superstition?"

"The church," she continued cautiously.

"There are those in the village who would like to see it left . . . undisturbed."

"You do want the church wall rebuilt?"

"Oh, dear," Mrs. Bell sighed. "I hope I haven't put you off. It's just that people talk, among themselves. You know how it is." She smiled weakly. "It's of no consequence, really. There's a meeting at the Society office at ten in the morning. I'll be 'round in plenty of time to take you over." With that, she turned and set off down the street.

Veronica looked at her mother. "What was that all about?"

"I'm not exactly sure." She frowned.

Once inside the house, a thorough search of the premises revealed a sunny kitchen with attached dining area, a large carpeted living room, and a wrought iron and wood staircase that spiralled to the second floor. Two wide bay windows looked out over a tiny garden filled with yellow roses, and a back patio that had just enough room for a few chairs, a table and a row of flower pots.

"I'll check the supplies down here," said Eddy, starting on the first row of kitchen cupboards. "You guys see what's upstairs."

"Don't forget your bags, you two," Mrs. Shaw called up the stairs after Ben and Veronica. "You'd better hang some of your clothes up—"

"Mom!" Veronica's terrified voice cut her short. "Come up here! Quick!"

Mrs. Shaw, followed by a nervous Eddy, burst into the bedroom to find Ben and Veronica staring at the dresser mirror. Across it, someone had scribbled a note in uneven red letters:

THE TREASURE HE GUARDS IS MINE!
BEWARE THE DANGER THAT LIES AHEAD.

CHAPTER THREE

Constable O'Toole squinted at the mirror. "Well, now." His Irish brogue filled the room like thick syrup. "I've been a policeman in this village for over thirty-five years and I've never seen the like of this before." He scraped a bit of the red crayon onto his thumbnail. "You found it just like this?"

"A silly joke that's not very funny," said Marion Shaw. "Do you have any idea who might have done it?"

"None at all."

"I do," said Veronica.

"Ah, yes," said the constable, removing

the folded yellow note from his tunic. "The gentleman on the plane. I'm not so sure the two incidents are connected."

"But they must be!" blurted Ben. "The messages are almost the same."

"And we saw him again in the airport after we landed," said Veronica.

"*You* saw him," reminded her mother. "The rest of us didn't."

"He was watching us, I know it."

"If you ask me," said Eddy, "I think it's got something to do with the old church Mrs. Shaw is here to restore."

The constable gave Eddy a long hard look. "It's true it's had its share of stories over the years."

"But what have they got to do with the restoration?" asked Ben. "Why would anyone go to all the trouble of breaking into a house to write a threatening message on a bedroom mirror?"

The constable stroked his chin. "You've obviously attracted someone's interest."

"Tell us about the legends and the curse," said Eddy.

"Well, there's the regular stories about ghosts and goblins and things that go bump in the night. You know what people are like —letting their imaginations run wild. They see and hear all kinds of things, or think they do."

"That's all there is to it?" asked Ben, disappointed.

"Ah well, now, I didn't say that, did I?"

The children looked at one another.

"The church dates back eight hundred years," the constable continued. "And there are some who believe the place harbors an ancient and terrible curse, carried through the centuries by a bloody ghost too dreadful to speak of." He lowered his voice mysteriously. "You'll find those who'll swear they've seen and heard this fearsome apparition."

Eddy gulped loudly. "Why does the ghost carry the curse?"

"Ah, well, that's where things get a bit fuzzy. No one seems to have an answer— only that it has something to do with royalty."

"Not much to go on," said Veronica.

"That's what legends are made of—stories, rumors and superstitions."

"Well," said Mrs. Shaw wearily, "we're not going to solve anything standing here. I have a meeting at ten tomorrow morning and some important reading to do." She glanced at her watch. "It's time you three got some sleep."

The constable snapped to attention. "Right you are, madam. You can rest easy, knowing I'm on the job."

After making a few more notes, he left Mrs. Shaw at the kitchen table with several reports spread out before her.

Ben, Eddy and Veronica trudged wearily upstairs and were soon sleeping soundly, tired out by the long journey and their mysterious introduction to the ancient village of Warlingham.

* * *

The next morning brought an excitement the three friends had never felt before—a strange, new land was waiting to be explored!

"We're going out to look around, Mom,"

Veronica told her mother right after breakfast.

"Be careful," warned Mrs. Shaw. "I'll probably spend most of the morning in meetings. I'll see you here for lunch."

The village of Warlingham was a bustle of morning activity. Cars and trucks sped by the green on their way to London. Doors jangled open as busy customers made their way from one shop to the next. Small groups of neighbors stood chatting with one another on the sidewalks. Everything in order—a small English village going about its business as it had for several centuries.

But Benjamin Hilton was puzzled. He was sure he'd seen several villagers whispering among themselves, pointing furtively at them as they passed. And despite Constable O'Toole, Ben was convinced the messages on the mirror and in Mrs. Shaw's pocket had been written by the same person. The handwriting looked almost identical. Was that person the man Veronica had caught watching them in the airport? Did the messages, as Eddy said, have something to do with the legend that surrounded the church? Was there a hidden meaning of some kind in Mrs. Bell's warning about disturbing the place?

"I've got an idea," he said suddenly. "I think we should get to know the layout of this whole village, street by street. There aren't that many and if . . ." He hesitated. "If we're being watched by someone, it wouldn't hurt to be ready. We might need any advantage we can get."

"Good idea," agreed Veronica. "Besides, it'll give us a chance to see the sights."

Eddy was shaking his head. "There's going to be trouble," he announced gloomily. "If you hang out with Ben Hilton long enough, it's bound to happen."

They spent the rest of the morning exploring every corner of the village, marveling over strange-sounding names, running their fingers over walls and statues and hedgerows that were centuries old, and crawling on crumbling stone fences that separated small green pastures from winding streets.

By eleven o'clock, the morning sun had all

but disappeared behind a canopy of drifting grey fog. Despite the change in the weather, the trio decided to follow the high street out of the village. At length, they came to a junction with a narrow lane that evaporated into the fog down a steep hill.

Ben looked at a tilting signpost above his head. "Baker's Hill Road," he read aloud. "Looks interesting."

"Looks like none of our business," countered Eddy. "Let's go back before we get lost."

But Ben was already halfway down the hill.

The road was indeed narrow and almost overgrown from lack of use. As the three explorers descended into the fog, towering oaks, dripping with moisture, closed in around them.

There was a sudden thrashing as a huge brown owl churned the silent mist above them in a flapping frenzy, before vanishing into the tangle of branches.

As he neared the bottom of the hill, Ben saw a dense wall of trees emerging before him, and realized the road took an abrupt turn to the right.

"Watch your step," he cautioned Eddy.

They were almost around the curve when they heard Veronica calling to them from somewhere in front. "There's water down here. I almost walked right into it."

Ben and Eddy moved carefully off the road until they found Veronica standing by the edge of a small overgrown pond. Oak branches draped with fingers of green moss hung over its stagnant surface. Wisps of fog prowled through reeds and over lily pads. With his toe, Ben flipped over a long-forgotten sign fallen face down in the deep grass. SLINE'S OAK POND was barely visible through the muddy stains.

"Spooky place," said Veronica quietly.

"And not one that appears to be any of our business," added Eddy.

He was about to turn back up the road when he heard the faintest of sounds. Slender wisps of fog swirled across the pond's surface, then stopped, as though pushed by an unseen hand. Hair prickled along the back of Eddy's neck. Slowly he lifted his eyes. Someone was standing on the far side of the pool, shrouded in the trees and mist. Someone with his head bent in shadow and his arms outstretched toward them.

It was the figure of a young boy.

Eddy glanced quickly at Veronica and Ben. They saw the figure too.

Suddenly the boy lifted his head, staring at them with pale sunken eyes.

"Listen!" said Ben. "He's crying."

The sound that had alerted Eddy drifted toward them across the pond, each wretched sob trailing away into the gloom.

"He's holding something," Veronica said. "I can't quite see what it is."

Then just as suddenly as the apparition had appeared, it vanished, dissolving into the dense cover of the trees beyond the pond. The whole incident had taken perhaps thirty seconds.

Eddy began to quiver. "Was that what I thought it was?"

"It must have been," said Veronica. "We all saw it."

"That's enough for me! I'm outta here!"

"Maybe it was just someone standing on

the other side of the pond," offered Ben as they followed Eddy to the top of the road. "Just because he looked spooky in the fog and everything doesn't mean he was a ghost—" He stopped suddenly, realizing what he'd said. "Wow! Do you really think he could have been?"

"Yes," said Eddy, hurrying along in front of them. "And I don't like it. Why did he have to pick me to haunt? Why isn't he where he's supposed to be? In an old castle or mansion or someplace like that? What kind of a ghost hangs around deserted swamps?"

"Ghosts haunt places where they lived," said Ben.

"Or died," Veronica added quickly.

"Give it a rest," whined Eddy.

They had reached the junction at the top of the hill when Ben stopped suddenly. "Eddy," he whispered urgently, "get back here!"

Only a short distance in front of them, a hunched figure hurried away along the road leading back to the village. The children's sudden retreat from the pond had caught him by surprise, and he'd not intended to be seen.

"Yipes!" Veronica exclaimed. "He followed us. Do you think he saw anything?"

"You can count on it," said Ben, confirming what he already knew — that their every move really was being watched.

"Didn't I tell you?" griped Eddy, looking at Veronica for sympathy. "Didn't I say it? If you hang around Ben Hilton long enough, something very nasty is bound to happen."

"Take a pill, Eddy," Ben said quietly. "What are you worried about? He's gone." He and Veronica were moving along the road again.

"You know as well as I do that's temporary. He's been following us ever since we got to England."

"That's a fact," nodded Veronica. "He's a creep on a mission, for sure."

"You promised me a vacation," continued Eddy dismally. "All you've done so far is scare me to death."

"We also promised your mother we'd be back for lunch," said Ben. "Let's have something to eat and decide what we're going to do next."

Eddy glanced around nervously, realizing suddenly that they'd left him standing by himself in the middle of the road. "Hey, wait for me!"

When they entered the kitchen on Glebe Road there was a note waiting for them on the counter.

SORRY ABOUT LUNCH.
EXTRA MEETING CALLED.
SANDWICHES IN FRIDGE.

They were almost finished the plate of sandwiches before Ben spoke.

"I've been thinking, if what we saw at Sline's Oak Pond was the ghost we've been hearing about, maybe somebody's written something about it."

"You mean in a local history?" asked Veronica.

"It's a possibility," he said, gulping the last of his milk and pushing himself to his feet. "Remember the library we saw this morning on the other side of the village?"

"It was pretty small."

"Yeah, but all libraries have local historical records."

Veronica nodded. "It seems like the right place to start." She and Ben were almost out the door.

Once again, Eddy realized he was about to be left behind. "Hey! Where's the fire? There's still two sandwiches left!"

The Warlingham Library consisted of a single room with three or four tables scattered about. The shelves were sparse, interspersed with several very large old paintings of historical figures. The only sound came from a heavy antique clock ticking solemnly on the end wall. Below it, three elderly gentlemen pored intently over copies of the *Times*.

"The children's books are against the south wall," a stern voice broke the silence. It belonged to a short, round woman with her hair swept back in a severe bun. Square spectacles rested delicately on the end of her nose. "You may take only three at a time."

"Thank you," said Ben politely, "but we

don't want children's books. We want to know about Sline's Oak Pond."

There was the slightest of movements behind one of the papers. A pair of eyes glared disapprovingly at the children.

The librarian shifted uncomfortably. "You're not from around here."

"We're visiting from Ontario in Canada," announced Veronica proudly. "My mother's the architect working on the church."

There was a significant pause. "What do you want to know about Sline's Oak Pond?" She peered at them suspiciously.

"Everything," answered Ben carefully, not wanting to give away too much.

"You'll have to be more specific," said the librarian. "The pond is mentioned in several historical records for this region. It's been there for hundreds of years."

"We're actually looking for something peculiar that might have happened there," said Eddy.

The room fell into a strained silence.

"Peculiar?" asked the librarian finally. "In what way?"

Ben realized Eddy was about to tell the librarian what had happened at the pond. He wasn't sure it would be wise to announce they'd just seen a ghost.

"Since we're going to be here for the summer," said Ben quickly, "we'd like to learn something about the local history."

"Well . . ." The woman shuffled uneasily back to her desk. "The Historical Society has put together these pamphlets." She gathered up a handful of material and handed it to Ben. "You're welcome to look through them but they must not leave the library."

With the papers in hand, the children seated themselves at a corner table. They were barely settled when Veronica noticed an open door leading to a small reading room. Seated at a heavy wooden table was a man partially hidden by a pile of oversized, hardcover books. He was writing intently, hunched over his work like an ancient monk. Veronica stared at him for several seconds before realizing Ben was speaking to her.

"There's nothing in these but tourist information. They won't tell us anything. We need to get—are you listening to me?"

"Ben," she whispered, "do you see that man?"

"Of course. So what?"

"He's the man who bumped into my mother on the plane! I'm sure of it."

The man's head appeared suddenly over the pile of books. For a split second his piercing black eyes locked onto the children in recognition. Before any of them could push their chairs back he was on his feet, through the door and halfway across the room.

At the library door he turned suddenly, leveling a menacing finger at the children. "You three brats are snooping around places you don't belong," he hissed. "Beware the ghost of Jonathan Matthew. His curse will be on your head!"

CHAPTER FOUR

"What we have here," said Ben, pacing up and down the front room, "is a jigsaw puzzle."

It was early evening. After spending several frantic minutes trying to follow the stranger from the library, the children had given up. He'd simply disappeared into the village's narrow streets and alleyways. Disappointed, the children had headed for home.

Now dinner was over, and Eddy and Veronica sat cross-legged at either end of the sofa. Marion Shaw stood in the doorway, her mouth set in a straight line.

"Here's what we know," continued Ben. "The first time we saw this guy was on the plane. That's when he must have planted the note on Mrs. Shaw. Then Veronica caught him watching us in the airport. That's two. And now we run into him at the library."

"Three," said Eddy.

"Don't forget about the message on the mirror," added Veronica. "That's four and a bit too much of a coincidence, as far as I'm concerned."

"Agreed," Ben confirmed. "There's no question he wants something that he thinks is somehow connected to us."

"That's the part that confuses me," said Marion Shaw grimly. "Warning me is one thing but threatening you children is another. I don't like it."

"But why is he threatening us?" asked Veronica. "That's what I don't understand."

"At the risk of sounding like a broken record," said Eddy, "I still think it has something to do with the work that your mother is doing."

"Like I said," repeated Ben, "a jigsaw puzzle—with a lot of pieces missing."

"We might be forgetting one of the key pieces in that puzzle," said Veronica. "Our mysterious friend's parting shot in the library."

"Jonathan Matthew," nodded Eddy.

"Who's Jonathan Matthew?" asked Mrs. Shaw. "Did you meet someone today?"

The children looked at one another. "Sort of," answered Veronica carefully. "We really didn't get a chance to talk to him."

"I don't understand. Was he unfriendly?"

"Cultural difference, I think," said Ben.

"Yes . . . well," said Marion Shaw, deciding it wasn't worth pursuing, "I have a big day tomorrow. The workers start dismantling the north wall and I have several calculations to make before that." She faced the three children. "I want you three close by because I don't trust this character one bit. You might be right—maybe he does have some connection with the project. I think I'll invite Constable O'Toole to drop around while we're working."

That was obviously going to be the last word on the subject for the rest of the evening.

Once her mother had retired upstairs to her work, Veronica suggested they play cards until bedtime. She set up a small table in the front room and hunted down some cards while Eddy made popcorn.

But Ben was edgy. He couldn't concentrate on the game, continuing to make one mistake after another. Finally, Eddy threw his cards on the table in disgust.

"All right, Ben, that's the fourth time you've trumped my ace. What's your problem?"

"I can't get the ghost of Jonathan Matthew out of my mind," said Ben uneasily.

"If that's who he really was." Eddy sounded doubtful.

"Our friend in the library seemed to know who he was," said Veronica. "And made it quite clear our presence wasn't required."

"That's a good point," puzzled Ben. "He warned us to stop snooping around."

"But we weren't snooping," said Eddy.

"We found the pond by accident."

Ben was pacing again. "Does he know that? Or does he think we're onto something?"

"And why would he mention the curse of Jonathan Matthew?" added Veronica. "What curse?"

"I don't know," Eddy answered wearily. "You saw the reaction we got from the librarian when we asked about Sline's Oak Pond. I think there are people around here who know more than they're telling."

Ben became thoughtful. "The threats could be a smoke-screen—just to scare us. Jonathan Matthew has something to do with what that man thinks we know. Is it a coincidence we were in the library at the same time?"

"Well," added Veronica matter-of-factly, "there's no question he wants something he thinks belongs to him. Remember the note on the mirror?" She hesitated. "Do you think we could be looking for the same information?"

"Why not?" Ben affirmed. "But for different reasons." He frowned. "I wonder what Mr. Personality is looking for?"

"Something that might have turned a young boy into an unhappy ghost," suggested Eddy. "A boy whose name might have been Jonathan Matthew."

"It looks as if all these things could be linked in some way," concluded Veronica.

Ben plopped onto the couch. "Our friend was certainly busy writing something down in the library this afternoon. I'll bet if we could see what it was, we'd have that link."

"No problem," said Eddy confidently. "Tomorrow we'll go back and have a look. The librarian will remember what book it was."

"Tomorrow will be too late," said Ben, getting to his feet. "If there's a connection between Jonathan Matthew and whatever that man is looking for, we'd better find out what it is before they start digging around the north wall of that church."

"Good point," agreed Veronica. "But there's nothing we can do about it tonight. It'll have to wait."

Ben had wandered to the front room

window and stood staring into the fog-shrouded darkness. "Not necessarily," he said slyly.

"Uh oh," Eddy moaned. "I've heard that tone of voice before and it's not good."

"Veronica?" asked Ben casually. "How would you like to go out for some ice cream? There's an ice cream shop at the far end of the green."

Eddy knew exactly what Ben was up to. "The one that just happens to be right across the road from the library?"

"Yes." Ben turned toward him innocently. "That one."

"Mom made it perfectly clear she wanted us to stay close by," warned Veronica.

"That's tomorrow. She didn't say anything about going out for ice cream on a lovely summer evening."

"Benjamin Hilton," said Eddy deliberately, "I know exactly what you're doing. You're using that ice cream as an excuse to get back to the library. How stupid do you think we are?"

"Let me see," Ben continued, ignoring

Eddy's outburst and turning his attention to Veronica. "If I remember correctly, your favorite flavor is strawberry."

Veronica grinned in spite of her misgivings.

"And if I'm not mistaken, Eddy's is chocolate."

"I'm not falling for one of your tricks, Ben, so you can give it up."

"Well," sighed Ben, "I guess it's just you and me, Veronica. I suppose we could always bring one back for Eddy."

"Mom!" Veronica called up the stairs. "We're going to the corner for some ice cream. We won't be long."

"Come back as soon as you're finished," came the reply. "I don't want you wandering around in a strange place after dark."

Eddy had parked himself stubbornly on the end of the couch, his arms crossed. He frowned at Ben. When his two friends were about to leave without him, he finally gave in.

"I suppose I'd better go with you. To keep you out of trouble," he added quickly. "Besides, you'd probably forget to put nuts on my cone."

* * *

If anything, the fog had become denser, swirling above them in the dark, making the already dim streetlights useless. It parted before them like a heavy curtain as they made their way toward the village green.

"I know this isn't likely to come as much of a surprise to you, Ben," said Eddy sarcastically, "but the library will be closed. Just how do you think you're going to get in?"

"I don't know," answered Ben. "But I do know we have to stay one step ahead of this guy. If we're right about him having some connection with the church, the curse of Jonathan Matthew has got to fit into it somehow."

"What if Jonathan Matthew is connected in some way? Then what?"

Ben shrugged. "It might tell us what the stranger is looking for, or what he seems to think we know."

"If nothing else," added Veronica, "it should confirm who Jonathan Matthew was."

"I hope you're not planning to do something stupid, Ben," said Eddy. "Like breaking in or anything."

They had passed most of the main street's darkened doorways and were only a few dozen steps from the shop, when Veronica stopped dead in her tracks.

"Look!" she whispered, flattening herself against the wall. "It's him!"

Through the shifting haze, the outline of the man who'd begun to dominate their lives stood out in sharp contrast to the blaze of store lights.

"For gosh sakes, don't let him see us," groaned Eddy, pushing himself in beside Veronica.

"We've got to follow him," said Ben.

"Are you crazy?" cried Eddy. "What if he turns around?"

"If we stay far enough behind, the fog will hide us."

"Ben's right," said Veronica. "We need to find out as much as we can about this guy."

"Keep dead quiet," said Ben, moving away from the wall. "He's starting up the street."

For several minutes the children followed the mysterious man, always near enough to keep him in sight, but never close enough to be seen or heard. Twice he turned, searching the fog as if he were listening for something. When he reached the corner opposite the library, he turned once more, then crossed the road quickly and disappeared between two huge gate posts.

"He's on the library grounds!" whispered Veronica in amazement. "You don't suppose . . ." She hesitated. "Why would anyone need to break into a library?"

"When he rushed out today," said Ben, "I saw him shove a piece of paper into his pocket. You heard the librarian after he was finished yelling at us. There's no way she's going to let him back in, ever! My guess is he didn't finish copying down whatever it was he found, and now he's come back to steal the books."

"Well, whatever he's after, he can find it without me," grunted Eddy. "I've had enough of this."

"Wait." Ben grabbed Eddy's arm. "He needs to get in and so do we. Why not let him do all the work?"

"Ben!" spluttered Eddy. "You said you weren't going to do anything stupid. This is stupid!"

"We'll be okay, if we're careful. But we have to get close enough to see what he's doing."

The eerie figure had stopped to raise his collar and turn down the brim of his hat. Then—

"Quick!" said Veronica urgently. "He's moving again."

As the man skirted the corner of the library, making his way to the rear of the building, the three children ducked behind the stone gates. Ben was about to hazard a cautious look when he felt a sudden familiar wash of frigid air. Every nerve became instantly alert.

"Jonathan!" he breathed hoarsely.

"What?" Eddy's ashen face followed Ben's gaze.

"There! At the far end of the green, do you see him?"

The pallid shape they had seen at Sline's Oak Pond stood unmoving beside a small clump of trees. Arms outstretched, it stared intently at them.

"Oh, no," moaned Eddy, "he's coming after us!"

"No," smiled Veronica calmly. "Looking after us, I think."

A sudden noise from the rear of the library caught their attention and when Ben turned back to face the green, the ghost of Jonathan Matthew had vanished.

"I'll bet he's looking for a loose window that can be forced open," whispered Ben, his attention back on the sinister man. "Let's go around the other side. Stay close to the ground and don't make any noise."

"He's probably got a gun," groaned Eddy. "Maybe I'll get lucky and he'll put me out of my misery first."

The side yard of the library ended at a low wood fence that was attached to the building's rear corner. As the children crouched against the wall deciding what to do next, they heard the sound of splitting wood. A sharp beam of white light swept across the lawn in front of them.

"Watch it!" warned Veronica. "He's got a flashlight."

Ben edged his way to the top of the fence and peered cautiously around the corner. The sound of a window being forced open made him drop back to the ground.

"He's breaking into the back room where we saw him this afternoon. We must've guessed right. Now we've got to figure out some way of seeing what he's up to."

"Maybe he'll leave the window open," said Veronica.

Eddy was incredulous. "You're not thinking of going in there!" he gulped. "At the same time as he's in there?"

"How else are we going to find out what he's looking for?" said Ben. "This was my idea, Eddy, and I'll take the chances. You two stay here and stand guard."

Eddy shook his head nervously. "You're leaving us out here by ourselves? Jonathan Matthew's probably got half the ghosts in England watching us right now."

Quietly, Ben climbed the fence and

dropped to the grass on the other side. On all fours, he crept slowly to a spot just below the window. After a moment's hesitation, he pulled himself carefully up by the ledge until he could see inside.

A flashlight lay on its side on an empty shelf, its pale beam casting a faint glow over the hunched figure at the end of the table. The man was writing again, scribbling furiously as his head moved back and forth between the paper and a heavy black book.

Ben realized his only hope of finding out what the man was copying was to get close enough to read the book's title. As quietly and carefully as he could, he hoisted himself over the window ledge and slithered silently through the opening to the floor.

For several minutes he lay perfectly still, listening to his heart pounding in his ears, convinced his forced breathing would give him away. Then, little by little, his cheek pressed hard against the rough floor, Ben threaded his way through a forest of chair legs until he had completed a large circle, ending behind the dark shadow at the table.

Again he froze, trying to control his breathing.

Suddenly, the figure half-stood as if to get up, then sat again to continue his work. Ben knew he would have to make his move now or forget it. Slowly, his heart planted firmly in his throat, he rose from the floor like a silent wisp of smoke, coming to his full height just behind the man's shoulder.

The flashlight was barely bright enough to show small dark figures on an aging page. Ben leaned forward slightly to bring the words into focus. He was almost close enough to read them when the entire room was flooded with the sudden brilliance of overhead lights.

Filling the doorway, his florid cheeks puffed out like red balloons, stood Constable O'Toole. His left arm was wrapped firmly around a squirming Eddy whose legs flailed helplessly against the air. His right held tightly onto the collar of Veronica's sweatshirt.

"WHAT IN THE NAME OF ALL THE

SAINTS OF IRELAND IS GOING ON IN HERE?!" he roared.

The startled stranger jumped to his feet, forcing the back of his chair into Ben's stomach. As Ben crumpled to the floor, the man leaped over the table, dove head first through the open window and disappeared into the night.

Ben struggled to his feet, gulping down great mouthfuls of air. "Quick!" he gasped. "He's getting away!"

"That's the man we've been telling you about!" yelled Veronica.

"And long gone he is, too," said the constable, his voice becoming suddenly stern. "Right now, you three have some explaining of your own to do. It's down to the police station with you."

As Ben made his way around the end of the table, his eye fell on a crumpled piece of paper almost hidden by the black book's cover. The stranger's notes! He quickly stuffed the paper into his pocket.

Perhaps they'd accomplished what they'd come to do after all.

CHAPTER FIVE

"We didn't break into anything!" insisted Veronica for the fourth time. "That awful man we've been trying to tell you about did the breaking in. All we did was follow him."

"A very foolish thing it was, at that," said Constable O'Toole, glaring at the three villains on the couch.

"Who knows what he might have been capable of doing," Mrs. Shaw added angrily. "If he had a gun or a knife . . ." She lowered herself heavily into the chair opposite the children. "I shudder to think of it."

"If I hadn't been on my usual round of the

village and seen the light through the library window, you three might not be sitting here right now."

"We were only trying to find out who he is," said Ben.

"It can't be important enough to risk your safety," Constable O'Toole insisted. "Besides, following people around in the middle of the night is my job."

Veronica watched her mother get to her feet again. Marion Shaw always stood when she had something important to say.

"Now, listen to me carefully," she began. "If you three don't want to be put on the next plane back to Canada, you'll do exactly as you're told. Is that understood?"

Ben, Veronica and Eddy nodded in unison.

"The work on the church begins tomorrow morning and I want you three sitting on the fence at the end of the churchyard, right where I can see you."

"But, Mom, we didn't do anything —"

"But me no buts, Veronica. Sit or fly. There are no other choices."

"Oh, all right. But I don't see why we

should be punished for something we
didn't do."

"And," continued Mrs. Shaw, "I think it
would be a good idea if Constable O'Toole
were to keep an eye on things tomorrow. This
character seems to have a bad habit of showing up whenever you children are around."

"I'd be more than happy to, madam," said
the constable. "But now that he's had a close
brush with the law, I rather doubt we'll see
him again. He'll disappear if he knows
what's good for him."

"We'd appreciate any time you can spare."

"A babysitter," muttered Eddy under his
breath. The comment got him a sharp jab in
the ribs from Veronica.

Ben didn't think it wise to draw any more
attention to what had happened in the
library. One of them, Eddy in particular,
might blab something. Better to let the
constable and Mrs. Shaw believe things
were under control, even though Ben was
convinced they hadn't seen the last of the
strange man. Right now he was interested in
only one thing—the yellow paper that lay

crumpled at the bottom of his jeans' pocket.

"You're right, Mrs. Shaw," he said agreeably. "We'll be happy to watch the excavation. It'll give us an opportunity to soak up some real live history." He yawned loudly. "It's been a long day. Time to hit the sack." He winked at Veronica, showing her just a corner of the note sticking above his pocket.

"Good idea," she responded quickly.

"Wait a minute." Eddy looked first at Ben then at Veronica. "What about the ice cream?"

"They're closed by now, son," said the constable. "You'll have to wait till tomorrow."

"Besides," Ben reminded him, "you always have nightmares when you eat ice cream before going to bed. Remember?"

Eddy had certainly had plenty of nightmares, but never from eating ice cream. He looked at Veronica curiously, realizing something was up.

"Well, I suppose it wouldn't hurt to get a good night's sleep. It has been a long day."

"A word of caution to you, my young friends," said Constable O'Toole. "There are families who've lived in this village for generations. Some have never left it—had no reason to. They like their traditions and customs the way they are—including their legends, if you know what I mean. They're suspicious of anyone who comes nosing around asking questions about this and that and upsetting things. Some don't take kindly to it at all." He paused then glanced at Mrs. Shaw. "Enough said. I don't see any reason to pursue this incident any further. I'll be on my way."

* * *

"Ice cream!" snorted Eddy. "I knew it was too good to be true." He sat on the end of Veronica's bed, staring dismally at his two friends. "What's with you two and your secret winks and signals?"

"Just a way for us to be alone," said Veronica. "Ben has something to show us."

From his jeans' pocket, Ben removed the crumpled paper and began unfolding its many wrinkles. "I have a feeling," he announced significantly, "that this is going to tell us what that stranger is up to."

Chapter Five

As soon as he saw the words written on the paper, Ben said, "That answers one question. It's got to be him who wrote the threatening messages. Look at the handwriting." He smoothed out the last creases, laying the page flat on the bed in front of them. "Who wants the honors?"

"I do." Eddy snatched up the paper. "I almost landed in jail because of this thing." He picked up the paper and began studying it closely.

"Well?" said Ben impatiently. "What does it say?"

"Strange spelling. It looks like he's been copying from a history book. Old English or something. He's translated some of it."

"Can you read it?" asked Veronica.

Eddy's brow knitted in concentration. "Most of it, I think. The first line gives a date — 1194, Wer-lyng-ham in Surrey. Looks like there used to be a bakery near Sline's Oak Pond."

"Baker's Hill Road!" said Ben excitedly. "We saw the sign this afternoon."

"And, it says, there was a boy who

worked at the bakery. He was on his way home one night when he was murdered."

"Wow!" gulped Veronica. "Pretty gruesome stuff."

"There's a note in the margin. Something about the Domesday Survey, dated 1193."

"I've heard of the Domesday Books," said Ben. "They were the first form of census-taking during the time of William the Conqueror."

Eddy's eyes suddenly widened in astonishment. "Look at this! One of the names on the survey is Jonathan Matthew, a baker's helper!"

"So that's how the stranger knows Jonathan's name," said Veronica.

"There's more," continued Eddy. "Villagers moved the boy's body to the church and placed it on the altar in preparation for burial. But before any arrangements could be made, the body disappeared, snatched by grave robbers."

"I remember reading about grave robbers in history class," said Veronica. "They were hired by medical schools. It was the only way students could get fresh bodies for their anatomy classes. It was quite common and very much against the laws of the church."

"It's too scary to even think about," said Eddy shakily. "I wish we'd never heard about Sline's Oak Pond, or Warlingham, or Jonathan Matthew."

"Some things are beginning to fit together," said Ben. "There's an obvious connection between Jonathan Matthew and the church, and that's probably why the guy on the plane is interested. But I still don't understand why he's threatening us."

"Did you read all the notes, Eddy?" asked Veronica. "Is there anything else?"

"Just a funny little diagram that doesn't make any sense."

About halfway down the page was a rough drawing of an extended oval with a cross-piece on it. Near its top was a jagged point, like a bird's beak, pointing toward the edge of the page. The words CURSE OF J.M. were written below the diagram.

"You're right," said Ben, handing the paper to Veronica, "it doesn't look like anything I've ever seen. What do you think?"

Veronica turned the diagram on its side then completely upside down. "Beats me." She shook her head. "There's only one person who knows what this means and he's not likely to tell us."

"I don't think we've seen the last of him, either," said Ben. "In fact, I'd be willing to bet you he isn't very far away right this minute, despite what Constable O'Toole believes."

"Lovely," said Eddy gloomily. "I'm going to sleep a lot better knowing he's out there waiting for me."

"If we only knew what it is he's trying to keep us away from," said Veronica earnestly.

"We know it has something to do with Jonathan Matthew's death," said Ben. "Otherwise, why would he have copied all that information down? And we can assume he's made some kind of connection between Jonathan's death and the church."

"Of course he did," said Veronica. "That's where the villagers took Jonathan's body. So what?"

"According to Constable O'Toole, the

legend says there were blood stains on the altar."

"And. . ." prompted Ben.

"I don't know. Maybe there's something valuable connected with Jonathan's death."

"You think that's what he's after?"

"Anything having to do with legends and stuff is always valuable," reasoned Eddy.

"Then why doesn't he just take what he wants and leave?" asked Veronica.

"Maybe he doesn't know where to look."

Ben studied his friend for a moment. "Eddy!" he said suddenly. "You're a genius! That's got to be it! He's waiting for the excavation work to begin at the church!"

"And that's what ties him to us," added Veronica. "Or at least to my mom."

"But," questioned Ben, "if he needs the excavation work, why is he threatening us? He's defeating his own purpose."

"He's using just enough tactics to frighten us but not enough to scare my mother off, at least not until he's got what he came for. He wants to scare us into giving him the treasure, if any of us get to it before he does, that's all. Remember the note on the mirror —The treasure he guards is mine," said Veronica.

"Now, wouldn't that be a real bonus—to find whatever he's looking for first," said Ben slyly.

"Right," smirked Eddy. "Just how do you propose to do that?"

"Since we've been grounded anyway, we'll be the first to see anything Mrs. Shaw happens to uncover."

"And you can bet our midnight prowler won't be very far away when the digging starts," said Eddy.

"That's okay. Mrs. Shaw won't have to worry about us, and Constable O'Toole will be dropping by to keep an eye on things. What could be safer?"

Eddy yawned loudly. "Now I really am tired. All this thinking has worn me out. I'm going to bed." Within minutes, he disappeared into his room and was curled into a ball, sound asleep.

Ben, however, was not so easily settled for the night. Wrapped in a blanket, he propped himself inside the window seat overlooking the street and let his mind ponder the incidents of the last few days.

No matter how he put the events together, the picture always came out the same— dangerous! The man who'd followed them to England had undoubtedly read the same newspaper story as Eddy's dad and was after something extremely valuable. It appeared nothing was going to stop him from getting it. Why were the villagers so nervous about the pond and the restoration work at the church? What exactly was the curse of Jonathan Matthew? And most important, what price would the four travellers now have to pay for being drawn into the intrigue?

The pieces of the puzzle swam through Ben's brain as sleep finally drifted over him. As his head fell back against the window frame, he imagined he saw a man in a raincoat and low hat standing between the stone gates of the library. His form was almost lost in the ghostly grey fog but his piercing black eyes stared intently at Ben.

CHAPTER SIX

Hour by hour, stone by stone, day by day, three well-behaved children watched from a low section of fence as the north wall of the Warlingham Church came down under the critical eye of Marion Shaw. The laborers worked slowly, removing the stones one at a time, setting them aside for eventual reconstruction. At the end of the second day, the wall was level with the churchyard, so work on the foundation could begin.

When the workers actually began removing the earth from around the stones at the base of the wall, each shovelful was lifted carefully and placed in a row along the edge of the excavation. More than once, Mrs. Shaw bent over the coarse soil, sifting it through her fingers, examining some small object that caught her eye. But after three days of painstaking digging, the men had come across nothing of significance.

As the work progressed, small groups of villagers gathered in the lane. They whispered among themselves, clacking their tongues and pointing.

By the end of the week, Eddy was beginning to wonder if they had made a wrong guess. "We've been sitting here for five days," he squirmed, "waiting for somebody to find something, and we haven't seen a thing."

"And our mysterious friend seems to have lost interest," added Veronica. "Not that I really miss him, but there hasn't been a sign of him since the work started. Maybe Constable O'Toole really did scare him off."

"Don't count on it," Ben warned. "He's around all right, probably doing exactly what we're doing—waiting."

"Speaking of Constable O'Toole," said

Eddy, "look who's coming through the gate."

The policeman headed straight toward the children, stopping only a moment at the wall of the church to inspect the work.

"Well." He puffed to a halt before them. "You three are finding all this quite fascinating, I'll warrant. Have you learned anything?"

"Yup," answered Eddy dismally. "I've learned I don't want to restore old churches for a living. Any new developments in the library break-in?"

The constable shook his head. "Queer business, that. The fellow seems to have vanished."

"Do you think we've seen the last of him?" asked Veronica.

"Hard to say. I gave his description to all the shopkeepers. They'll keep an eye peeled for him, you can be sure of that." He groaned, stroking his chin. "There was one strange thing last night . . ."

"Strange?" asked Ben, leaning forward.

"Sort of. Old Mr. Woodson over on Purley Lane—he's ninety-six, lived here all his life.

He rang me up about eight o'clock and said he'd had a visitor, a history professor. The gentleman was asking questions about the church."

"What kind of questions?"

"Something about the legend and, oddly enough, questions about an ancient artifact of some kind. Mr. Woodson remembered the library was broken into and thought he'd better tell me about his visitor."

"Did you get a description of the man?" asked Ben excitedly.

"Couldn't." The constable pushed his cap back on his forehead. "Old Woodson's blind. Has been for a few years. I doubt if it has any connection with the library break-in. We've always had people nosing into our local history. Could have been anybody."

Veronica, Eddy and Ben exchanged glances. They knew this had been no casual tourist asking idle questions.

"It looks like they're finished for the day," said Eddy, jumping to the ground.

It took the workers a few minutes to gather their tools, cover the stones with plastic sheeting and get the construction site ready for the next day's work. Marion Shaw spent the time doing sketches of the building and taking notes. She finally tucked her pencil into her clipboard and headed across the yard to the children.

"We're making good progress," she said proudly. "It won't be long before the restoration can begin."

"Mom," asked Veronica casually, "have you found anything . . . unusual around the foundation?"

"Unusual?"

"Anything that looked valuable or really old?"

"Nothing at all." She smiled at her daughter. "Planning to become an archaeologist?"

"Just curious."

As they moved out of the churchyard, the fog seeped in around them, cloaking the pathways in a grey woolly blanket so thick it twisted in folds around their feet. At a small take-out shop in the green, they stopped to buy fish and chips wrapped in newspaper.

Dusk descended over the village bringing

the streetlights to life, their frail yellow fingers barely able to penetrate the gloom. Several times, Eddy caught glimpses of black bats flitting in and out of the pale overhead glow. Their silent, shadowless forms made him think of the dark stranger.

Since their arrival in England, his activities had caused them no end of worry. His persistent warnings were very real and, Eddy was convinced, meant to be taken seriously. He thought for a moment about the incident in the library and realized how close they'd come to being in real danger.

But now it looked as if the man had disappeared. Or had he identified what it was he was looking for, and was simply waiting for the right moment? Was he watching them from the edge of the fog this very moment, following, threatening, planning his next move? Eddy stared into the darkness and shivered.

"I have a project report to write," said Marion Shaw, turning up the driveway. "Why don't you make popcorn and watch TV for a while?"

Watching television was the last thing on Ben's mind. He was thinking about Mr. Woodson's visitor and Constable O'Toole's belief he had no connection to the library break-in.

As soon as they were inside, Ben looked at Eddy and Veronica. "Conference," he said urgently, starting up the spiral staircase.

Once the three were comfortably seated on Veronica's bed, Ben pulled the stranger's crumpled paper from his pocket.

"Did you hear what Constable O'Toole said about Mr. Woodson's visitor?" he asked earnestly.

"Asking questions about the church," frowned Eddy.

"Exactly. And we all sensed that was no history professor." He held the paper up. "He knows about Jonathan Matthew's connection to the church and the curse because he threatened us with it."

Eddy and Veronica looked bewildered.

"Think about it," said Ben. "What did Jonathan Matthew have in his hand at Sline's Oak Pond?"

"Looked like a stick or a metal rod or —" Veronica's eyes suddenly widened in amazement. "Do you think . . . the artifact!"

"Right on. I'll bet that whatever it was Jonathan was carrying is what the stranger is after. That's why he was asking questions."

"You've lost me," said Eddy, shaking his head.

"Remember the legend," continued Ben. "After the villagers carried Jonathan's body to the church, they went away to make funeral preparations."

"But before anything could be done," added Veronica, "Jonathan's body was snatched by grave robbers."

Ben held up the wrinkled paper. "Take another look at this diagram in the margin. Could that be a poorly drawn picture of a valuable piece of English history?"

Eddy stared at the drawing. "Maybe. But what is it? Why is the ghost of Jonathan Matthew wandering around the countryside waving it all over the place?"

"That," said Ben excitedly, "is what we

need to find out. It has something to do with what happened to Jonathan the night of his murder—the stealing of his body from a sacred place. Do you have any idea what that thing would be worth to the right buyer? There are people who'd pay a fortune for an object that old just to say they owned it."

"You mean he wants to steal it so he can auction it off to the highest bidder?"

"Something like that."

"Those kinds of historical items belong in museums where everyone can enjoy them," Eddy protested.

"It's also illegal," Veronica added. "My mother's told me about people who've gone to jail for stealing artifacts." She shook her head. "But I don't think our friend is too worried about that."

"What's important now," said Ben, "is finding out what that object is and how it's connected to Jonathan."

"And getting it before that thief finds it," said Veronica.

"Good luck!" Eddy snorted. "He obviously

knows more than we do and that gives him a definite advantage."

"With some luck," said Ben, "we might be able to get a little help from old Mr. Woodson. And from Jonathan Matthew himself."

Veronica raised an eyebrow, looking sideways at Eddy.

"What if Jonathan's appearance at the pond was his way of asking for help?" continued Ben. "You saw the way he held his arms out to us, like he was pleading."

"Help?" repeated Eddy. "How do you help an eight-hundred-year-old ghost?"

"By offering him some peace and quiet . . . and a permanent resting place. There must be a reason he's been wandering for so long, and I bet it's connected to the curse."

"But we don't know anything about the curse, not really."

"That's where old Woodson comes in. The stranger heard the story of that artifact from someplace—a rumor, an old history book— and believes he's onto something big. He ends up at Mr. Woodson's, the local historian, trying to find out as much as he can. Why can't we do the same? We're going to need the information when we meet Jonathan Matthew again."

Eddy's eyes bugged out of his head. "Wait a minute! I'm not sure I heard that right. Did you say 'when we meet Jonathan Matthew again'?"

"Of course. How else can we help him? I'm convinced Jonathan Matthew appeared to us on purpose because he needs our help. We need to learn exactly what the legend is really about, find the artifact before the stranger does, and put the ghost of Jonathan to rest for all time."

Eddy shrugged at Veronica in disbelief. "Sounds simple enough to me."

"Let me get this straight," said Veronica carefully. "You want us to go looking for Jonathan? Where do you think we'll find him?"

"At the church," said Ben confidently. "He came to us at Sline's Oak Pond and we saw him again near the library. There's no question he knows our every move. So I'm convinced he'll find us at the church, too. After all, it is where the villagers took his body."

There was a moment of silence before Eddy said, "You've come up with hairy ideas before, Benjamin Hilton, but this one tops the list."

"Maybe not," said Veronica thoughtfully. "Maybe Jonathan wants someone to understand him, to take the burden of eight hundred years from his shoulders."

"There's not much chance he'll show himself around a churchyard full of workers in broad daylight," said Eddy. "You can forget that."

"Who said anything about broad daylight?" asked Ben casually.

Eddy glared at him. "If you think you're going to get me into that churchyard, with all those graves, in the fog, in the middle of the night to go ghost hunting, you're a crazy person."

Ben was a picture of innocence. "Did I mention going anywhere?"

"You didn't have to," insisted Eddy. "I can

hear the wheels going around in that warped little head of yours."

"We'll never get away with it, Ben," Veronica agreed seriously. "If we get caught again, my mother will have us on a plane faster than you can blink."

"Look," reasoned Ben, "the church is just through the park at the end of the street, five minutes away. We'll be there and back before anyone knows we're gone."

"The whole thing should be turned over to the police," said Eddy unhappily.

"You heard what Constable O'Toole said. He doesn't think there's any connection between Mr. Woodson's visitor and the library break-in."

"Ben's right," sighed Veronica. "He wouldn't pay any attention to us at all."

Eddy wrung his hands. "I don't like it. The last time we fell for one of your half-baked ideas we almost ended up in jail."

"But we got what we went for," Ben pointed out.

"And now you want to go ghost hunting in a graveyard at midnight."

"We need to find that artifact before you-know-who does and leaves the country with it."

There was a moment of silence while Veronica and Eddy looked at one another, then at Ben.

"I don't suppose there's any hope of trying to talk you out of this little scheme?" asked Veronica.

Ben shook his head. "Not unless you've got a better idea."

"Well," she gave in, "let's get on with it. It sounds like it's going to be a busy night."

As quietly as possible, the three detectives slipped through the kitchen door and across the back garden to the fence.

"Purley Lane is four streets over," said Ben. "I saw the sign for it last week when we were exploring the village." He glanced at his watch. "It's only seven-thirty. We've got lots of time to talk to Mr. Woodson and still get some sleep."

At the bottom of Purley Lane, a decaying wooden sign propped against a crumbling gatepost identified the Woodson residence.

An angular thatched cottage, barely visible through the trees, sat at the end of an overgrown walkway.

"Looks awful quiet," said Veronica. "Maybe we should think about coming back another time."

"Yeah," agreed Eddy, "like next year."

"There's no time left," said Ben, starting toward the house. "The worst he can do is ask us to leave."

The first knock at the door brought no reply. But a second much sharper one got an immediate and irritated response.

"I'm blind, not deaf!" the raspy voice shouted from inside.

Another moment passed before the door opened and the children came face to face with the oldest human being they'd ever seen. Mr. Woodson's lined face made him look at least a hundred and five. He carried a bent cane which he waved wildly in front of him, as if poking his callers with it might help identify them.

"Who is it this time? Can't an old man get any peace?"

Twice the cane smacked Eddy lightly on the side of the head before he could take a step backward out of its reach.

"We're sorry to bother you, Mr. Woodson," Ben began.

"You're not sorry at all," the old man yelled. "Or you wouldn't be knocking my door down. Who are you? What do you want?"

"My name's Ben Hilton. My two friends and I would like to talk to you about the curse of Jonathan Matthew and—"

"Ah! The Canadian pests. Yes. I know about you, Ben Hilton and Veronica Shaw and . . . and . . . the other one. Mucking around the church. I hear things, you know. The affairs of Jonathan Matthew are best left alone."

"But we want to help him," Veronica interrupted.

"And there's a man trying to steal an artifact," added Ben, hoping to get the old historian's attention.

Mr. Woodson's cane came to rest. He took a step forward, cocking his head to one side as if listening intently to Ben's voice. "What do you know about that?" he asked in a low rumble.

"Only what we've been able to guess. That's the reason we're here—to get the whole story from someone who really knows."

There was a moment of silence while Mr. Woodson gave the children's request careful consideration. "Well, don't just stand there," he grated suddenly. "Come inside. We've got talking to do."

The interior of the cottage was dim. The only light in the front room came through a small window facing the lane. It spilled gloomily over walls, bookshelves and table-tops covered with newspapers and historical documents.

Eddy stared at the papers, wondering how a blind man could read what was in them. He was about to ask but hesitated suddenly. From somewhere in the room's dark recess he heard the faintest of sounds. A whisper? A sigh? He glanced quickly at Ben and Veronica. Nothing. Had he imagined it? No. There it was again. This time he recognized it — a barely audible sob. He's here! thought Eddy, terrified. He's in this room!

"So, it's the story of Jonathan Matthew you want."

Dribbling tobacco over the blackened edges of his pipe bowl, the old historian settled comfortably into his favorite chair. "You're the second in as many days."

"We know," said Ben. "We think the man who came to ask you questions before is a thief."

"You know about the treasure, then?"

"Only what the constable told us," said Veronica. "We thought you'd have told the strange man the rest of the story."

"I told him nothing! I knew he was up to no good. Had a dishonest voice."

Ben hesitated before he spoke again. "Will you tell us the story?"

The old man chuckled. "Don't see any reason why not. You said you want to help Jonathan Matthew?"

"Yes," Eddy said, "help him find peace

after eight hundred years."

The historian took a long draw on his pipe, and nestled so deeply into his chair that he looked like a wizened dwarf.

"Well then," his voice croaked in the near darkness, "listen closely to one of the best kept secrets in all of England—the true story of the curse of Jonathan Matthew.

"It is the year 1194. The third Holy Crusade is over. King Richard the first, nick-named The Lionheart, a formidable foe with a reputation as an unyielding conqueror, has returned once again to England.

"But even kings have their family secrets. Some historians—I am one of them—believe that in the years before the third crusade, Richard had taken under his care a young woman with an infant son. He provided them with money, food and a place to live near the castle gates."

"Why would he have done that?" asked Eddy suddenly.

"The reason for his generosity is unknown. But as the boy grew, he and the king became like father and son. They read together, chased rabbits and hunted deer through the forests, and learned to love and respect one another. Then with the flurry of tactical planning and preparations surrounding the coming crusade, the two had less time to spend together. During the next six years, the young woman and her son were neglected, replaced by the battle-fields of the Holy Wars.

"On the night of Richard's return to England, his thoughts once more turned to the boy he had not seen for more than six years. He sent two of his soldiers ahead to determine the child's welfare while he rested at an inn in County Kent.

"For ten days the soldiers searched the countryside, asking questions about the woman and her son. Finally, they discovered the two had settled here—in the village where you and I now sit—called then, Werylingham in Surrey. The woman kept a small house while the boy worked nearby as a baker's helper."

"Baker's Hill Road," nodded Ben.

"The very same." The old man dug into

his pipe bowl, emptying its contents into an ashtray. "The soldiers soon made the king aware of their discovery. But the news was not all good. On their way out of the village, they gave chase to a wagon driven by two men believed to have snatched a body from the local church—the body of the baker's boy who'd been found earlier that same night lying on the road outside the village. The boy had been brutally murdered by a madman with an ax and carried to the church by villagers who had laid him on the altar table."

"Jonathan Matthew," Veronica said grimly.

"During the chase, the robbers threw Jonathan's body into Sline's Oak Pond where it sank out of sight."

"We saw him there!" said Eddy excitedly.

"Many have seen him, my boy, or think they have." Veronica shivered.

Mr. Woodson once again fussed with his pipe. "You can imagine Richard's distress when he learned the fate of the young man he'd grown to love like a son. He demanded to be taken to the church, to the altar where the villagers had placed Jonathan's body. There he knelt to pray for the boy's soul. Before he left, he placed his dagger on the very spot where Jonathan's blood had stained the altar, and swore that should the dagger ever be removed from its place, Jonathan's spirit would bring a terrible curse to bear upon those responsible."

Eddy was mesmerized. "That's what Jonathan was holding in his hand at Sline's Oak Pond! That's what the curse is all about!"

The old man nodded. "But only those who've been in the churchyard or near the pond on New Year's Eve will swear they've seen the dagger."

"New Year's Eve," reasoned Ben. "The night of his murder."

"Others believe he carries a piece of the ax that killed him," Mr. Woodson went on, "or his own hand, hacked off during his struggle with the murderer. This village has lived under the threat of that curse ever since." He sighed deeply.

"A handsome weapon it was, hand-forged from the finest steel available, with many precious stones set into the handle and cross-piece. It was a gift from the king's father. Never once had the dagger been out of Richard's sight. Of everything he owned, he valued it the most."

"Now an artifact of incredible value," said Ben.

"For centuries, treasure hunters have sought that dagger," continued Mr. Woodson, "Jonathan's only link to the one man who ever really loved him like a father, Richard the Lionheart, King of England."

"What happened to the dagger after the king left?" asked Veronica.

"Later that same night, there was a terrible storm. Part of the church roof collapsed into the chancel, destroying everything below it. The dagger was probably lost in the rubble."

"No wonder some of the people in the village want the church left undisturbed," said Ben grimly. "They're afraid the curse will descend on them."

"You were right, Eddy," said Veronica. "That man's hoping my mother will find the dagger so he can steal it."

"But how does he know what he's looking for?" asked Ben.

"He doesn't," the old historian said slyly. "Not sure. Hundreds of years of rumors and half-truths have created the legend. They're all he has to go on."

Ben was suddenly on his feet. "Then we have to find it first!" he announced excitedly, reaching for the old man's hand. "Mr. Woodson, you've been just great!"

"Forget it, Ben," said Eddy, laying the historian's pipe carefully in its ashtray. "We wore him out. He's sound asleep."

By the time the three made their way back to the lane behind the house on Glebe Road, it was dark.

"Who's for getting some zzz's?" asked Veronica sleepily. "It's going to be a long night."

Eddy was working up a good protest, but before he had a chance to speak, Ben was through the door and on his way upstairs.

"I'll set my watch for twelve-thirty to

make sure everything's quiet, then I'll wake you."

Long after Ben had gone to sleep, Eddy lay staring into the darkness of the bedroom. His thoughts wandered to his mother's kitchen where the sun streamed through the yellow curtains and the smell of freshly baked cookies hung on the air. He wondered if she missed him, wishing with all his heart he was home, sitting on the counter, watching her work . . .

Then someone was shaking him out of his dream.

"It's time to go!" whispered Ben urgently.

CHAPTER SEVEN

For several minutes, Ben, Eddy and Veronica threaded their way through silent village streets. Then they turned onto a road that narrowed until it was nothing more than a pathway, ending by the gatehouse at the churchyard entrance. Attached to the gatehouse was an arch smothered in dark green ivy.

Here the three intruders stopped, staring apprehensively at the scene before them.

The Warlingham Church was a strange and forbidding sight by night. The decaying stone building loomed out at them, its jagged bell tower outlined sharply against the night sky. Moss-laden branches from grotesque oaks hovered like clutching fingers over the grave markers that hugged the church walls. The older stones were sunken, distorted by the weak light. Dozens of others stretched away into the drifting mist.

As they moved into the dark recess of the yard itself, small night sounds reached the children's ears. Mice scurried through the deep grasses, the soft cooing of doves floated above them; and from some invisible distant corner came an owl's throaty hoot, adrift on the damp night air.

"This is not my idea of a fun night out," whispered Eddy nervously.

"We need to find a spot where we can see most of the churchyard," said Ben. "Some-place that's well hidden but still lets us see anything that moves."

"There's a walkway along the east wall," said Veronica. "Mom told me about it. And a small garden with a bench in it. We can probably see the whole churchyard from there."

"Good. Lead us to it."

The three picked their way carefully through the maze of grave markers, stepping over and around fallen stones. Most of the yard was untended, taken over by the undergrowth. Once, Eddy caught his foot on a vine and almost pitched straight forward into the gaping darkness of a freshly dug grave.

"Here's the path," said Veronica finally. "And there's the garden." She pointed to a small square set into the surrounding vegetation. "The bench is on the far side."

Ben walked to the center of the space and turned in a complete circle. "It's perfect. Between the three of us, we'll be able to watch the whole yard from here."

"We can't just sit here all night," complained Eddy. "How long are we going to stay?"

"As long as it takes," said Ben, arranging himself comfortably in the middle of the bench. "You two can sit on the ends and cover the front and back. That way we can't miss him when he comes."

Veronica looked at him doubtfully. "You seem awfully sure Jonathan Matthew is going to show himself. What if you're wrong?"

Ben shook his head. "Take a look around you." He stared into the surrounding gloom. "It's a perfect night for a ghost."

"Even if we do see him," said Eddy, edging a little closer to Ben, "what then? Do we just walk up and say, 'Excuse me, but would you like to tell us where the dagger is hidden'?"

"I doubt if we'll have to worry about that," answered Ben seriously. "He'll know what to do."

Eddy drew his jacket tighter around his shoulders and settled back on the end of the bench. "I've said it before and I'll say it again," he muttered. "You're a very sick person, Benjamin Hilton."

That ended the conversation. The three watchers sat silently, their eyes scanning the grey mist as it rolled over the cemetery and through the trees. Occasionally, a wandering breeze sent the fog climbing the dripping stones of the church wall, creating eerie shapes against the gothic windows.

After half an hour of searching, Eddy's eyes grew heavy. His head fell forward and Ben soon heard the sound of regular breathing. A few minutes later, Veronica followed, her head coming to rest on Ben's shoulder. By shifting his position, he could manage to see most of the churchyard. He decided not to wake his friends.

Another thirty minutes passed and Ben found his own concentration beginning to waver. He had almost decided that their vigil was a waste of time and was about to wake Eddy and Veronica, when a dark form near the gatehouse wall caught his attention. He stared at it intently for several seconds, saw it shift quickly to the right along the church wall, then disappear around the corner.

"Wake up!" he whispered sharply.

"What?" stammered Veronica.

"I just saw something move near the end of the wall."

Eddy jerked upright. "What's happening?"

"Shh! We've got company." Ben pointed to the spot where the side wall of the church met the back wall under the bell tower.

"Are you sure?" Veronica strained her eyes. "I don't see anything."

"Maybe it was just the fog," said Eddy uneasily.

"I don't think so. It was too dark and moving too fast." He was about to stand up when the clouds above them parted, flooding the entire churchyard in a sudden wash of brilliant white moonlight. Trees, gravestones and the sinister shape of the church itself stood out in stark relief from one another.

"Wow!" exclaimed Veronica in a breathless whisper. "It looks like the set for a horror movie!"

Ben was pointing again. "Keep down!" he said urgently. "There it is again."

This time the form came into full view, moving stealthily along the church wall. A high collar and low-brimmed hat told the children exactly who they were watching.

"Oh, no!" said Eddy. "Not again!"

"Do you think he knows we're here?" asked Veronica.

"Not likely," answered Ben, flattening himself against the ground. "And we'd better keep it that way."

The stranger stopped about halfway down the wall, turned and surveyed the yard. Here he dropped to his knees and began digging frantically with his hands.

"What's he up to?" asked Eddy curiously.

"He's looking for something."

For several minutes they watched as the man scrabbled and grunted at the base of the wall. Finally he stood and removed a short iron bar from his inside coat pocket. This he wedged tightly between two stones.

"It looks like he's trying to rip the stones out!" gasped Veronica.

She had barely finished speaking when there was a dull grating noise and like magic, a low section of the church wall swung suddenly outward.

"An opening!" Eddy almost jumped to his feet. "How did he know it was there?"

"Any archaeological diggings or alterations made to ancient buildings have to be recorded," said Veronica. "I learned that from my mom. He must have found some old records when he was at the library. I'll bet the church has been renovated before, and that opening got blocked off then."

The stranger glanced about him once more, then, crouching, entered the opening's inky blackness, where he disappeared downwards.

"Neat trick. There must be a tunnel. Where do you think it goes?"

"There's only one place it could go," said Ben getting to his feet. "Under the church. C'mon, let's check it out."

But before Ben could move, Eddy grabbed his arm. "Tell me you aren't thinking about following him down that hole," he said anxiously.

"We came here to find that dagger. We all agreed how important it is."

"And we're not important? We've already had one close call with that character."

"He's right, Benjamin," agreed Veronica. "If that guy ever gets his hands on us, we're done for."

It was logic Ben couldn't argue with. They'd been warned by both Mrs. Shaw and Constable O'Toole. But the mystery that had begun at Sline's Oak Pond with the appearance of Jonathan Matthew fascinated him. Benjamin Hilton was on the trail of something he wasn't about to let go.

"Look," he reasoned. "We have the advantage. He doesn't know we're here and we can probably find out what's going on by listening at the opening. We're so close! We can't just turn around and leave, not now."

"You wanna bet!" said Eddy emphatically. "There's nothing I'd rather do than walk through that gate and forget this whole thing."

"Well," said Ben casually, "I suppose if you want to walk around all those gravestones, in the dark, by yourself, and take a chance of falling into an open grave—again —go ahead. I can't stop you."

"Aww, Ben," Eddy moaned. "Did you have to bring that up?"

"He does have a way with words," grinned Veronica.

"We'll have a quick look and leave," said Ben, sensing victory. "Veronica, you and Eddy circle around to the left side of the door. I'll go to the right. Watch where you're going and keep quiet."

As they split up, Ben dropped to all fours and scampered in a wide arc toward the dark opening in the wall. He had almost reached the north corner and Marion Shaw's excavation work when the stranger's form suddenly appeared in the doorway. Ben ducked behind a large headstone and watched as Veronica and Eddy did the same.

The man quickly retrieved the steel bar he'd left lying on the ground and disappeared again through the opening.

The three reached the wall at the same time and began edging their way toward the door until they stood on either side of it. Slowly Ben bent forward and cautiously peered around the opening into the darkness. The faint sounds of scraping rose into the night air.

"Digging again," he whispered. "And he must have a flashlight. I can see light coming from somewhere." He pulled back. "We have to find out what he's doing."

"Ben," warned Veronica, "down there

isn't the same as being in the library with him. There's only one way out."

"I'm only going to look."

"Famous last words," nodded Eddy. "We should let Constable O'Toole catch him red-handed."

"By the time we persuade Constable O'Toole to come, it'll be too late. And what if he tells Veronica's mom what we're doing?"

"I'd rather take my chances with her than our friend here," mumbled Eddy.

On his knees, Ben moved around until he faced the opening. "There's no steps, just a drop to the ground. Grab my ankles and lower me through until I signal you to stop. And whatever you do, don't let go!"

Complaining constantly under his breath, Eddy sat with his legs braced against the church wall and took hold of Ben's ankle. Veronica did the same on the other side. Together they slid Ben over the lip of the opening into the pit.

At first Ben could make out nothing; the darkness was too complete. But somewhere ahead of him, off to the right, the sound of the metal bar scraping on stones and dirt grew louder. His eyes picked up the faint glow of the flashlight, casting eerie shadows over fallen beams and chunks of misshapen rock. He wiggled his foot indicating he wanted up.

"I can't see anything from that angle," he said, dusting himself off. "I'm going to have to go right down there to find out what he's doing."

"Ben!" Eddy protested.

"It's okay. He's digging near the north wall close to Mrs. Shaw's excavation. There's no chance he's going to see me. I could feel the floor with my hands. It's only a bit below the opening."

"Then I'm going too," said Veronica suddenly.

"Wait a minute," gulped Eddy. "What about me?"

"You can stay here and be our watchdog," suggested Ben. "Warn us if anybody comes."

"Forget it! I'm not staying up here by myself with the ghosts and the bats. I'm going with you."

First Ben, then Veronica and finally Eddy lowered themselves carefully onto the dirt floor below the foundations of the church.

It took a few minutes for them to adjust to the dim light before they began climbing over beams and around stones toward the sound of the digging. Ben took the lead, picking his way slowly from one obstacle to the next, turning after each one to make sure Eddy and Veronica were behind him.

They moved at a snail's pace but finally Ben came to an abrupt stop before a huge flat slab of stone. One end rested on a second vertical stone. The other end was half-buried in the dirt floor.

"Look at this!" he whispered excitedly. "An altar stone."

"Probably fell through the floor from above during the storm Mr. Woodson told us about," observed Veronica. "It must have been left here after the church was restored. You can see the outline above where the floor was replaced."

Eddy was brushing dirt away from the altar's surface. "There are stains all over the top. It almost looks like—"

"Dried blood stains!" said Veronica in a hushed voice. She ran her fingers gingerly over the rough surface. "This is probably the original altar where the villagers put Jonathan's body."

"No wonder there are stories surrounding this place," said Ben shakily.

So engrossed had the three explorers become with their find that they failed to notice that the digging had stopped. The light in the underground chamber became suddenly brighter as a dark shape wielding a flashlight leapt toward them. Before they could make a move, the figure scrambled past them over several fallen beams and slithered through the low door to the churchyard above.

"I've got you this time, you nosy brats," he hissed, his outline filling the opening. "Once this door closes, it's all over for you three. Jonathan Matthew will finish you for good!"

With horror, the children watched as the stranger placed all his weight against the stone door, moving it slowly inward toward its original resting place.

"He's going to bury us alive!" shouted Eddy hysterically.

"Quick!" yelled Ben. "Help me find something to wedge in the opening!" He and Veronica searched frantically.

But things were happening too fast. The opening became quickly smaller until the door slammed suddenly into place, plunging the children into the pitch blackness of a tomb. The sound of the crashing door echoed and vibrated through the surrounding stone—fitting music for a desperate situation.

"I think he's really done it to us this time," said Veronica quietly. "I guess we really shouldn't have messed in things that don't concern us. We were warned."

"Are you all right, Eddy?" asked Ben.

"I suppose," came the answer after a short pause. "I can't move the door at all. He's wedged something against it."

"There's got to be another way out of here."

"Don't count on it. Even if there was, how

would we find it? I can't even see my hand in front of my face," came Eddy's mournful voice.

Ben began probing the air in front of him, hoping to touch something he would recognize. He was about to suggest they move close to one another so as not to get separated, when he felt an icy breath sweep over him once again. In the next instant, the outlines of Eddy and Veronica appeared before him bathed in a soft radiance.

"Veronica's right," continued Eddy with forced enthusiasm. "He's really done the big one on us this time. If I had my choice, I'd rather spend two hours alone with Jonathan Matthew's ghost."

"You might get your wish." Ben's terrified whisper was barely audible. "He's standing right behind you."

CHAPTER EIGHT

Marion Shaw paced back and forth between the couch and the front room window, wringing her hands in desperation. Constable O'Toole stood in the doorway, his notepad open and his pen poised.

"Now, Mrs. Shaw, keep calm and tell me exactly when you realized the children were missing."

"I told you," she answered impatiently. "I worked late and went into Veronica's room just before one in the morning. She was gone. They were all gone, all three of them." She stopped pacing. "It has something to do with that man who's been following them. I know it has and I'm worried."

The constable glanced at his pocket watch. "I'm sure they can't be very far away. This is a small village and it won't take long to search it, especially not at two-thirty in the morning, with nobody up but us."

"I'm not going to forgive Veronica for this," Mrs. Shaw said grimly.

"Can you remember anything they might have told you, anything that might give us a clue about where they've gone?"

"I insisted they stay close to the church during the renovations and I don't think they ever left the churchyard."

"I can attest to that, madam. I saw them there myself this very afternoon when I told them about—" The constable rubbed his chin. "Hmm, I wonder . . ."

"What is it?"

"Probably nothing. I was telling the children about old Mr. Woodson over on Purley Lane. He'd had a visitor asking questions about the church. Your Veronica was very curious about what kind of questions. When

I mentioned something about a missing artifact, young Ben got quite excited."

"Artifact? What artifact?"

"Seems the visitor wanted to know something about an ancient relic connected with
the church."

"Wait a minute!" said Marion Shaw
suddenly. "Just before we left the churchyard this afternoon, Veronica asked me if
I'd found anything unusual around the
foundation, anything that looked old and
valuable." She exchanged glances with
Constable O'Toole. "I think we'd better have
a little chat with Mr. Woodson and find out
exactly what kind of nonsense he's been
feeding those children."

* * *

Ben's words hung on the still underground air
like the announcement of a death sentence.

"T-this is n-no t-time for j-jokes, Ben,"
stammered Eddy, his terror surpassed only
by his inability to speak. But even as he
stumbled over the words, he felt the hair
prickle along the back of his neck and he
knew Ben was not joking about the ghost.

The thin white light was seeping quickly through the darkness, filling the entire room with its smouldering radiance. Both Eddy and Veronica stepped fearfully back toward Ben.

The apparition was as Eddy had first seen it, bowed head partially hidden in shadow. A blood-stained shroud, draped around his hunched shoulders and falling in loose folds, ended just above his ankles. The glow spreading out behind him swirled and flickered like a disturbed candle flame. Then, as if being awakened from a long sleep, the ghost raised his battered head, and fixed his pale sunken eyes on the trembling children. For several long moments, the specter stood perfectly still in the deep silence of the cavern.

And then it was the sound that filled the children with real dread.

At first it was nothing more than a tender whimper, so full of sorrow and grief that Ben was sure he'd never heard anything so pitiful. But its intensity swelled, gathering volume until it was a howling wail of desperate misery, echoing and re-echoing from the walls of their stone prison. The soul of Jonathan Matthew cried out, as if the curse itself was about to materialize before their very eyes.

Eddy felt himself begin to panic. "What does he want?!" he screamed, covering his ears.

And then there was silence. As the last traces of Jonathan's lament bounced from stone to stone, he suddenly raised his arms, stretching them toward the children as though pleading.

Ben took a step forward. "He wants our help. Look how he's reaching out to us."

"What kind of help can we possibly give a ghost?" asked Eddy nervously.

"Remember the legend," said Ben. "Before funeral arrangements could be made, grave robbers stole the body."

"What's that got to do with anything?"

"For one thing, he never had a proper burial," said Veronica. "That's why he wanders the countryside haunting the places where he lived."

Eddy stared at the glowing figure. "Wow!" he gulped. "Sort of like having no home."

"And after eight hundred years of worrying over a dagger that everyone seems to want to steal . . ." Ben gazed at the figure before him. "Well—you tell me how desperate you'd be?"

"He's come to us for help and we can't let him down." Veronica's voice was urgent.

"What does he expect us to do about it?"

"Jonathan's spirit will come to rest once he knows the dagger is safe from thieves," Ben continued. "I'm sure of it!"

"When we saw him at Sline's Oak Pond he held the dagger out toward us," said Veronica. "Now he doesn't have it."

"Maybe he lost it," suggested Eddy.

"I doubt it," said Ben. "Maybe he can only carry it on special occasions—like New Year's Eve. Besides, in eight hundred years, there's no way we're the first ones who've tried to get that dagger. You can bet he knows where it is. Maybe he's testing us, to see how far he can trust us."

"Wait!" said Eddy excitedly. "Look!"

Jonathan's ghost had moved further back into the recess of the chamber, and stood beckoning them, his arm making great circular motions in the air.

"He wants us to follow him!" said Ben.

"Follow him where? What if we get lost down here?"

Veronica looked at Ben. "Eddy's right. We don't know where this thing might lead us."

"But he's come to us for help. Why would he want to hurt us?"

The ghost was beckoning them deeper into the maze of rock and broken timber, and Ben was not going to be left behind. "C'mon," he urged. "What choice do we have?"

For the next several minutes, they clambered over beams, around chunks of stone and through curtains of grey cobwebs as they followed the glimmering shape. At one point, Veronica's foot slipped, wedging her between two huge blocks of wood. It took Ben and Eddy several minutes of wiggling and pulling to free her. When they looked up, the nebulous form of Jonathan Matthew was still there, patiently waiting.

"You see," said Ben confidently, "if he was

going to hurt us, he'd have done it by now. He's had lots of opportunity."

"I'll believe it when we're out of here," Eddy grumbled, "not before."

"I hope my mother hasn't discovered we're missing," said Veronica. "She'll be worried sick."

"When she gets her hands on us," said Eddy wryly, "sick will take on a whole new meaning."

Ben halted suddenly. "He's stopped."

"Look!" pointed Veronica. "There's a stairway. I think he's showing us a way out."

The spirit had come to rest at the foot of a set of ancient stone steps set against a wall. The stairs appeared to climb to the ceiling of the underground room and simply end there.

"Great," said Eddy. "Just what we need. A stairway that doesn't go anyplace."

"But it must be there for a reason," puzzled Veronica. "At some time, it must have gone somewhere."

Then, without warning, the shrouded specter of Jonathan Matthew began to rise, gliding upward step by step until it disappeared through the ceiling, leaving the children in complete and silent darkness.

"Any more bright ideas?" asked Eddy after several moments had passed.

"Veronica's right," insisted Ben. "The stairs must be there for a reason. Something's been covered up and maybe we can find it."

Feeling his way through the dark, Ben found the first step and began working toward the top until his hands brushed against the ceiling.

"Hey!" he shouted. "There are wood planks up here. And I can feel . . . an outline of something, maybe. I bet it's an opening! If you two want out, you're going to have to work for it."

Crowded together on the top step, the three friends clawed and pushed against the thick boards. Dust that had filled cracks for hundreds of years rained down over them. Several times they stopped to cough and clear their eyes. Finally, one of the wide boards shifted and a thin strip of white light fell across Ben's arms.

"They're moving!" he grunted breathlessly. "We're almost there. One more push should—"

Suddenly, the entire structure collapsed. Floor boards, clods of earth and loose rock rained through the opening, exposing the prisoners to the grassy churchyard above. Eddy was the first to climb through. He flopped onto his back, sucking the cool night air into his lungs. Veronica and Ben were soon beside him and for several long moments the three lay perfectly still staring into the moonlight.

"Ghost hunting is for the birds," said Veronica finally. "Especially underground ghost hunting."

"Speaking of ghosts," said Ben, rolling onto his stomach, "ours seems to have disappeared."

"Who cares?" Eddy frowned.

"He showed us a way out," Ben reminded him. "And he didn't do us any harm."

"After all that," said Veronica wearily, "we're no further ahead. We haven't found the dagger, we still don't know who this strange character is who's been following us, and now we don't even have a ghost. The more I think about this whole thing, the more tired I get."

"And to top it all off," griped Eddy, "we almost got buried alive."

"Stop complaining," said Ben. "I'm thinking."

"That," said Eddy, getting angrily to his feet, "is our major, number-one problem. When you think, we get into trouble. I, for one, have had enough. No more mysterious ponds or churches or ghosts in bloody rags, or underground passages." He jabbed his finger at Ben. "And no more sneaking around in the middle of the night with an eleven-year-old idiot who thinks he's Sherlock Holmes."

With determined strides, he headed across the yard. He'd almost reached the entrance to the gatehouse when he came to an abrupt halt. Striding down the road beyond the archway, her arms swinging with each purposeful step, her fists clenched and her mouth set, was Marion Shaw.

Behind her, Constable O'Toole struggled to keep up.

CHAPTER NINE

Veronica Shaw was curled into a corner of the living room couch, her head bowed, her arms folded loosely in front of her. The figure towering over her was steaming mad.

"What do I have to do to keep you out of trouble, young lady? Handcuff you to the porch railing? Lock you in your room and throw away the key?" Marion Shaw began to pace. "I can't leave the three of you alone for one hour without you wandering off in the dark someplace." She turned suddenly. "Just what were you doing in that cemetery in the middle of the night?"

It was Ben's turn to feel uncomfortable. "That was my fault. Veronica and Eddy had nothing to do with it. We were looking for something . . . valuable." He hesitated. "Something we have reason to believe is buried under the church."

"That something wouldn't happen to be a jewelled dagger, would it?"

Veronica's mouth dropped open. "How do you know that?"

Marion Shaw and Constable O'Toole exchanged glances. "When I discovered you were missing I called Constable O'Toole. We put two and two together and paid a short visit to Mr. Woodson, trying to find out exactly what his mysterious visitor had wanted to know. Among other things, Mr. Woodson told us the complete story of Jonathan Matthew. That's how I found out about the dagger. It's only a legend of course, the kind of thing the tourists eat up. We never for a moment thought you three would take it seriously."

"But it's true!" Eddy exclaimed. "We've seen him."

"Seen who?" asked the constable.

"Jonathan Matthew, of course," added Veronica. "We saw him at Sline's Oak Pond the second day we were here and again tonight at the church."

"Veronica," said her mother patiently, "if Jonathan Matthew existed at all he would have died almost eight hundred years ago."

"We know that. That's why we went to the churchyard in the first place, hoping his ghost would lead us to the dagger before —"

"Before it gets lost forever," Ben interrupted quickly. He gave Veronica a warning glance. It wouldn't be a good idea to tell Mrs. Shaw and the constable about their adventure with the strange man beneath the church foundations.

"Are you telling me you three have been out ghost hunting in a church cemetery in the middle of the night?" asked Mrs. Shaw sternly.

The children's guilty looks were the only answer.

"Very foolish," said Constable O'Toole looking from one face to the next, "very foolish, indeed. Might have tangled your-selves in a hedge or fallen into an open grave."

Ben gave Eddy one of his I told you so looks.

"And what if you'd run into that creep who's been bothering us?" Mrs. Shaw shook her finger at them. "He may have been the very man who visited Mr. Woodson."

"I've had no reports back from any of the shopkeepers," said the constable. "He's not been seen since the incident at the library. It's my feeling he's gone for good."

It appeared to Ben as if things were going back to normal — at least as far as Veronica's mother and Constable O'Toole were concerned. Neither of them were prepared to believe that Jonathan Matthew or his ghost were anything but the products of vivid imaginations. That, Ben reasoned, was probably good. And the constable's belief that they had seen the last of the mysterious stranger seemed to make Mrs. Shaw feel better about their safety.

As far as the legend was concerned, the whole thing was beginning to feel like a very bad dream. Eddy was right, they'd all had just about enough of midnight cemeteries, weeping ghosts and ominous threats. If this mystery was ever going to be solved, there were some questions that needed answers.

Was it possible that the legend was only that—a legend? Was there really a curse? And if there was, did that mean that an eight-hundred-year-old ghost needed to be laid to rest? The questions buzzed around Ben's tired brain like hungry mosquitoes. He had to know the answers, once and for all. Ben knew they had to come up with a plan, a plan so clever it would solve the riddle beyond the shadow of a doubt.

In his mind, just such a plan was beginning to take shape.

* * *

The next morning it rained and the work at the church was postponed. After three hours spent at the kitchen table with her notes, Mrs. Shaw suggested Eddy and Ben call home to chat with their parents.

Eddy called first, and in less than five minutes his mother was in tears. She told him how much she missed him, and worried that he wasn't eating properly or getting enough rest.

"Stop blubbering, Mom, I'm fine," he insisted.

Alison answered the phone at Ben's house to inform him that Mom and Dad had gone out to a movie and that she had dropped his brand new ghettoblaster down the basement stairs. Ben hung up on her.

By two o'clock the rain stopped and the children were getting restless. They were not used to sitting around doing nothing. Finally, after several failed attempts at various games, Ben suggested they go for a walk. The plan he'd been working on needed some input from the other two. He wanted to talk to them alone.

"We might be grounded," said Veronica. "But I'll check it out."

She returned moments later and informed them that if they were gone for longer than one hour, her mother would phone the airline office and buy three one-way tickets to Canada.

"Pay attention, Benjamin Hilton," said Eddy. "That little bulletin was for you."

Several times on their way down Glebe Road, Veronica glanced at Ben. His brow was wrinkled in thought and she knew he was hatching another scheme.

"What's up, Benjamin?" she asked finally.

"I think there's a way we can force our mysterious friend into the open, make him play his hand."

Eddy stopped dead in his tracks. "Haven't you learned anything in the last twenty-four hours?"

"I've got a plan," Ben held up his hands. "Let me finish. What if he thought we had the dagger, that we'd found it under the church?"

"What he thinks is we're three corpses drying out in that underground tomb," said Veronica wryly.

"Exactly. He'd be more than a little surprised to find out we escaped—with the dagger."

"You're forgetting one small detail," said Eddy. "We don't have it. We don't even know where it is. In fact, we don't even know if it exists."

"Does it make any difference, as long as our friend doesn't get his hands on it?"

"That's what I tried to tell you yesterday," said Eddy. "Why bother?"

"Because," continued Ben seriously, "this character's a dangerous thief. He broke into our house and into the library. He makes threats and tries to kill people. He's got to be stopped before he does someone some serious damage."

"You're right about one thing," agreed Veronica. "He's definitely dangerous. How do you plan to get him into the open without getting us all killed?"

"All we have to do is get a dagger from an antique store, any old replica. Then, figure out some way to make him believe we're going to put it out of his reach for keeps. If he thinks he's going to lose it, he might get desperate enough to do something stupid."

"Not bad," said Veronica.

"And, if Constable O'Toole just happens to be around when he's needed . . ."

"There are a couple of problems."

Veronica shook her head. "How do we let him know we've got the dagger and, more important, that we intend to keep it away from him?"

"That part's got me stumped," said Ben, scratching his head. "We can't risk getting too close."

"Why should that be a problem?" said Eddy.

"How do you figure?"

"He knows every move we make. Just carry it around till he sees us with it."

"Sounds too easy," Veronica frowned.

"Wait a minute!" said Ben suddenly. "That might work if—" He looked at his two friends intently. "What do you bet he'll go back to the church looking for the dagger?"

"Maybe," said Veronica doubtfully. "What are you getting at?"

"As far as he's concerned, we're done for. That means your mother's restoration work will come to an end and he'll have to do his own digging if he wants that artifact badly enough."

"And all we have to do is be in the right

place at the right time so he sees us," added Veronica.

"Right," affirmed Ben. "With the dagger in hand."

"This is getting ridiculous!" interrupted Eddy. "I don't believe what I'm hearing. You can't be seriously thinking of going back into that churchyard."

"Yes!" continued Ben excitedly. "But this time *we're* going to be in control, instead of Mr. Nasty."

"Famous last words," moaned Eddy.

"What about my mom?" asked Veronica suddenly. "We might as well start packing our bags when she finds out what we're up to — and she will find out."

"I'm counting on it," grinned Ben.

The Warlingham Antique Store's doorbell jangled merrily overhead as the children entered. Immediately, a pleasant round face peered through a curtain at the back of the narrow shop.

"How may I help you?" asked a tall, grey-haired woman.

Chapter Nine

"We're looking for an . . . antique," answered Ben, glancing around him at the hundreds of objects that lined the shelves and window ledges. Some looked as though they hadn't been moved in years.

"What kind of antique? I have many."

"A gift," said Veronica, "for a friend in Canada."

"A letter opener," Ben added. "Do you have any?"

"Liar," muttered Eddy under his breath.

"As a matter of fact, there are some right here." She produced several from a cupboard drawer. "Aren't they lovely?" she chirped.

"We'll take that one," said Ben. "The big one in the middle with the rhinestones in the handle."

After the shopkeeper wrapped the opener carefully in newspaper, the children left the store and started for home.

"What makes you so certain the stranger will go back to the churchyard?" asked Eddy suspiciously.

"Because he knows that as soon as Mrs. Shaw and Constable O'Toole put two and two together, that churchyard will be crawling with people looking for us. That doesn't give him much time. He's desperate."

"Making him all the more dangerous."

"And more careless," added Veronica. She thought for a moment. "Ben, what happens when he sees us?"

"Yeah, genius," piped Eddy sarcastically. "What's the big plan for getting the bad guy under control?"

Ben regarded his two friends seriously. "I think I've got that figured out. It's going to take some careful timing and a lot of help from you two."

CHAPTER TEN

As Ben, Eddy and Veronica reached the top of Glebe Road, the rain began again in earnest. By the time they arrived at the back door, they were soaked to the skin.

Mrs. Shaw stood at the front window staring into the bleak afternoon. "Rain, rain, rain," she sighed. "We won't be getting anything more done today, I'm afraid."

Just as well, thought Ben. We need the time for planning. He nodded Veronica and Eddy toward the stairs.

In less than five minutes, Ben was into dry jeans and a T-shirt, waiting impatiently with paper and pencil for the other two to get changed. When they were all comfortably in their familiar circle on the bed, he began.

"First things first. Are we all agreed that we're doing what needs to be done?"

"Since when did you start worrying about that?" grumbled Eddy.

"Because this plan needs teamwork. Timing is everything."

"We're in," said Veronica confidently.

"Good!" He drew a large square on the paper. "Here's the churchyard and here's the wall with the secret door. We were sitting here." He made a small circle to represent the garden with the stone bench and several lines indicating the paths that led to it. "We know about three openings into the church-yard—here, at the main gatehouse by the road. Another one here, through the hedge at the bottom of the graveyard. And the small gate right here, behind where we were sitting. It leads to the open field."

"There's got to be more," said Veronica.

"Likely. But if we don't know where they are, he probably doesn't either."

"Why are the openings so important?" asked Eddy.

"When he finds out we're not under the church, he'll be confused. That gives us the advantage. And when he sees the dagger, he'll do anything he can to get his hands on it. We'll play a little game of hands-off with it—up and down the paths, and through the gravestones. But if something goes wrong, we'll need escape routes to get out of there. He'll be so mad he won't know which way to go."

"Mad enough to kill the first person he catches," said Eddy.

"Mad enough," corrected Ben, "to get caught red-handed by Constable O'Toole."

Veronica and Eddy looked at one another in amazement. "How do you plan to do that?"

"Easy," said Ben. He turned toward Veronica. "Your mother will go straight to Constable O'Toole as soon as she checks and finds us missing. All we have to do is leave a note telling her where we are."

Eddy rubbed his chin uneasily. "I don't

know. There are a lot of things that could go wrong. What if Mrs. Shaw doesn't see the note in time? What if our friend catches one of us while we're trying to keep the dagger away from him?"

"Nothing can go wrong," insisted Ben. "Believe me, it's going to work like magic." He was suddenly off the bed. "Veronica, get a piece of paper and write a note for your mother. Just tell her we know where the mysterious stranger is and what he's up to, and to bring Constable O'Toole to the churchyard. Eddy, get some towels and pillows together and stuff them in the closet. We'll make the beds look like someone's sleeping in them."

By mid-afternoon, they had gone over the details of the plan several times. Everything was set, and the children wiled away the rest of the day watching television. More than once their attention was distracted by the wind and rain driving against the windows as if in grim anticipation of what was to come. This was it. There would be no more chances.

At supper, Mrs. Shaw studied each face closely. "You're a quiet bunch," she said finally. "What's up?"

"Nothing," answered Ben casually.

"I hope you three haven't made any . . . arrangements for the evening." She looked directly at Veronica. "You do know what I'm talking about?"

"Yes, Mom. We get the picture."

"Then, if you don't mind doing the dishes, I'll get back to my paperwork."

"She knows something," whispered Eddy a few minutes later. "She knows what we're up to."

"She suspects we're up to something, all right," agreed Veronica. "I told you, she's hard to fool."

"That's okay," said Ben. "It means she'll check on us to make sure. We want her to find us missing at just the right time."

"I've got this horrible feeling again that you don't know what you're doing," said Eddy dismally.

By the time Mrs. Shaw tossed her pen onto the table in front of her, it was already eleven-thirty and the children had gone to bed to read. She looked in on Veronica first, then the boys, before they heard her close the door to her own bedroom down the hall.

"I figure she'll be back at least twice," ventured Ben quietly.

Fifteen minutes later, he watched Marion Shaw's head peer around the opening and disappear again. He waited until he heard the click of her door before he shook Eddy.

"Time to go to work," he whispered, pulling his jeans on. "Get the stuff out of the closet and make these beds look like someone's in them." He wedged the letter opener carefully into the front of his jacket. "I'll get Veronica."

He tiptoed carefully into the hall, noticing with satisfaction there was still light coming from under Mrs. Shaw's door.

Veronica was already dressed, busy jamming some towels and a pillow under her sheets. "Here's the note." Her voice was barely audible. "I'll leave it right on the floor in the doorway."

Within minutes, the three adventurers

were making their way up Glebe Road toward the green and along the lane that led to the church. The village was deserted, silent except for the distant barking of a lonely dog. The wind and rain had given way to the familiar grey fog that crawled stealthily in front of them. Somewhere to their left a door slammed.

At the end of Church Lane, the gatehouse became visible through the drifting curtain.

"Timing is everything," Ben reminded his two companions. "If we get separated, remember where the escape routes are."

Like a setting from Dracula, the church-yard was a blend of shifting shapes and leaden shadows. Gravestones folded into the surrounding fences and hedges, rain-soaked trees loomed over the uneven paths, and the stone walls of the church rose like sentinels guarding a sanctuary for the uncaring dead. The scene brought the three friends to a halt beneath the gatehouse arch.

Ben turned to Veronica. "You'd better take the lead since you know the way."

"This place gives me the total creeps,"

moaned Eddy nervously as they again threaded their way through the maze of tilting gravestones and overgrown paths toward the stone bench. More than once, Ben stopped abruptly, listening for any sound that would warn them of the stranger's presence.

They had barely reached the small circular garden when Eddy dropped suddenly to one knee. "Look!" he whispered urgently. "The door in the wall, it's open!"

"He must be here already." Ben glanced around quickly. "Get down behind the bench and don't make a sound."

As if in response to Ben's guess, the dark shape of the stranger emerged through the opening, flattening itself against the stone wall of the church. He was wearing a long raincoat and low-brimmed hat. A crowbar dangled loosely from his left hand.

"You were right, Ben," whispered Veronica. "He's been digging again."

"And has undoubtedly found out we're not where we're supposed to be," added Ben.

The figure's head shifted from side to side uneasily, as if trying to decide what to do.

"He's confused," said Ben eagerly. "Let's help him make up his mind." Before the other two knew what was happening, Ben jumped onto the bench seat waving the fake dagger above his head. "Looking for something?" he called ominously.

The figure at the wall crouched fearfully at the sound of the strange voice then rose slowly, staring in disbelief. "You!" he raged. "How did you —"

Eddy was terror-stricken. "Ben! What are you doing?"

Ben's plan was in full swing. "Veronica!" he shouted. "Take the path we just came down. Eddy, go off to the right and stop near the tree."

The stranger made his move. He charged toward Ben, the crowbar raised threateningly over his head.

Ben jumped to the ground. "Handle first, Eddy. Don't miss!" The letter opener made a perfect spiral into Eddy's waiting hand.

The figure suddenly changed direction.

"No!" he screamed. "Don't let it fall!"

Airborne again, this time the opener flew over the stranger's head into Veronica's outstretched hand.

"That's it!" yelled Ben. "Keep it away from him!"

Again the stranger spun on his heels in a vain attempt to follow the fake dagger. "You brats will regret this," he growled menacingly.

As Ben moved off to the right, Eddy headed back around the bench, ready for Veronica's throw. The dagger sailed through the air, caught the reaching tip of an oak branch and tumbled end-over-end toward the ground—out of Eddy's grasp! At the same instant, his toe caught under a vine, sending him forward in an uncontrolled roll. He made one complete somersault, coming to rest on his face and chest, gasping for air.

Ben's first thought was to rescue the letter opener. He changed direction in mid-stride, ran between Eddy and the oncoming stranger, and scooped it into his hands, narrowly escaping ten clawing fingers.

The stranger charged past Ben and pounced on Eddy like a vulture, dragging him to his feet.

"You miserable little pest," he snarled. "I'm going to teach you a lesson you won't soon forget!"

Eddy was terror-stricken. "Put me down! Put me down!" He struggled desperately.

Quickly, Veronica positioned herself behind the stranger, waving her arms frantically to get Ben's attention.

"The dagger!" she cried. "Throw me the dagger."

As the letter opener sailed over his head, the man dropped Eddy like a sack of laundry. He leapt into the air, missing the spinning blade by the tiniest margin. It landed safely in Veronica's hand.

Instantly, Eddy was on his feet and out of the stranger's reach. "Run!" he shouted. "Before it's too late!"

With the dagger lodged firmly under her sweater, Veronica headed for the gatehouse with Ben and Eddy at her side. They lurched over loose cobblestones and vaulted over gravestones, never daring to look back. As they passed under the gatehouse arch, Ben chanced a glance over his shoulder. The stranger wasn't exactly on their heels but he wasn't giving up either. He had the trio well in sight.

"I thought this was where the cavalry was supposed to arrive," wheezed Eddy.

"Things happened too fast," puffed Ben. "I didn't expect him to get to the church before us."

"It seems you didn't expect a lot of things — as usual."

"That's history," said Veronica. "The question is, what do we do now? We're almost in the village."

"We have to dump this guy for openers," labored Eddy. "I can't run much longer."

"The pond!" said Ben suddenly. "We'll lose him at Sline's Oak Pond."

"But that gets us further away from help," Eddy protested.

"He'll chase us as long as he thinks we've got the dagger."

"There's no time to argue about it now,"

said Veronica urgently. "Make up your minds. He's getting closer."

They had reached the crossroads where Church Lane met the high street and Baker's Hill Road. It was decision time. Ben knew there was no chance of trapping the stranger in the village. Trying to get the thief anywhere near Constable O'Toole would be useless. The stranger would simply disappear to wait for the next opportunity and their whole plan would be for nothing. If they were going to snare him, it would have to be on their terms, on their ground, with their rules.

"Come on," he shouted, turning his back on the last feeble street lamp. "It's the only chance we've got."

As the three figures disappeared over the brow of Baker's Hill Road, the silent swirling fog swallowed them completely.

At the bottom of the hill, they stepped off the road into the cover of the oaks.

"Now what?" gulped Veronica, crumpling wearily to the ground. "We can't hide down here for long. He'll find us."

"If your mother checked our bedrooms once more," said Ben hopefully, "at least she'll know we're out here . . . someplace."

"Another one of your brilliant plans gone astray," said Eddy dismally. "She's probably sound asleep."

The crunch of hurried footsteps on the gravel came to a sudden stop directly opposite where the children crouched in the trees. Eddy was convinced they'd been seen and was about to make a break for the top of the hill. Suddenly, the footsteps moved on down the road and around the bend toward the pond.

"Now's our chance!" he whispered excitedly. "Let's get out of here."

"Wait," Ben held him back. "He has no idea where we are. That gives us the advantage."

"To do what?"

"When he realizes he can't find us, he'll leave. We'll follow and find out where he's hiding. I'm sure that'll get Constable O'Toole's attention."

Carefully they crept back onto the road,

staying well behind the retreating footsteps below them. Several times the sound stopped, only to begin again a few seconds later. Finally, it stopped altogether.

Since they'd started down the road the fog had lifted somewhat, pushed aside by a slight breeze that swept over the trees and into the small clearing by the pond. Filtered moonlight turned the surface of the water into a ballet of shifting patterns and creeping fog. Silence surrounded them completely.

"Have we lost him?" Veronica's voice was barely audible. "I don't hear anything."

A sudden explosion of sound and shadow erupted at the pool's edge. The stricken children froze in terror as the stranger's sinister form rose from the long grass, his coat spread like the wings of a giant bat, his piercing eyes stabbing at them from under the brim of his hat.

"This is it, brats," he snarled, "the end of the line." As he reached his full height, a hand clutching a large black pistol emerged. Pointing it directly at the threesome, he spat the words out one at a time. "I want that dagger, and I want it right now."

"Take one more step," said Ben in a voice he'd never heard before, "and the dagger goes into the pond. You'll never see it again." He held the prize behind his head like a baseball ready to be delivered to home plate.

"Who wants it first?" came the threat. The gun swung toward Eddy. "How 'bout the nervous one? Should I shoot him full of holes so you can watch him sink into the mud?"

"Give it to him, Ben," screamed Eddy. "He's not fooling! He'll shoot me for sure!"

"I doubt it," countered Ben warily. He knew the gun would soon be leveled at him instead. For the moment however, they were at a standoff.

"Now look, kid," the man took a menacing step forward, "I'm not in any mood to play games." The gun moved from Eddy to Ben. "Either I get what I came for or somebody won't live long enough —"

The sound began as a faint rumble, like the first stirring at the edge of a thunderstorm . . . and it grew, spreading through the air over the far side of Sline's Oak Pond.

The stranger lowered the gun, turned to face—what? His eyes flicked from one side of the pond to the other, searching, straining to find the source of the sound.

Veronica shuddered suddenly. "Look!" She pointed above the dark oaks near the water's edge.

Ben's stomach turned to putty. In the distance, high above the trees, a foaming ash-grey cloud came rolling across the heavens. At first it appeared to have no definition, no form; but as it swept toward them, shapes began to emerge.

A pair of horses, staring and wild-eyed, boiled through the haze, whipped to a frenzy by two drivers sitting high on the seat of an ancient clattering wagon. The animals' screams and the sound of their pounding hooves filled the black air.

Then, as if sighting its target, the wagon dipped suddenly below the level of the trees and hurtled across the water toward them. Two flickering yellow lamps danced wildly from each side and the sharp snap of a whip cracked through the night sky.

Eddy dropped to his knees, his head buried in his arms. "Get down! Get out of the way! It's coming right at us!"

"What is it?!" the stranger screamed. "What are you brats up to?!" He waved the gun wildly over his head, firing in all directions.

The vision swept up the side of the pond and bore down upon them. At the last possible second, when Ben was certain they would be crushed in a driving mass of churning hooves, the wagon veered sideways, tilting on its edge to reveal its terrible cargo.

Standing in the wagon box, his blood-soaked shroud trailing in fluttering rags behind him and his pallid sightless eyes staring into the night, was the corpse of Jonathan Matthew! Above his head he clasped the prize the stranger had worked so hard to find.

"The dagger!" cried Ben.

The wagon made a sharp turn, rising over the children's heads, twisting abruptly toward the man holding the gun. In the same instant, Jonathan Matthew's ghost hurled the dagger. It flashed through the air, handle first, striking the gun-wielding stranger squarely on the forehead. His weapon exploded once more before arcing over the slope and disappearing into the dark water of Sline's Oak Pond.

The horses leaped onward, carrying the wagon with its ghastly specter over the horizon above Baker's Hill Road where it vanished as quickly as it had appeared.

Ben stood frozen in the sudden silence. Jonathan Matthew had accomplished his task. The stranger lay on the ground in an unconscious heap.

In the confusion, Ben had dropped the letter opener. It was nowhere to be seen and he assumed it had met the same fate as the stranger's gun.

"Can I look yet?" asked a frightened Eddy. "Is it gone?"

Veronica picked up the dagger, rubbing it gently between her thumb and forefinger. "Hard to imagine all this fuss over a piece of steel."

The night air was suddenly filled with voices. Constable O'Toole, with Marion Shaw and several villagers close behind, rounded the bend at the bottom of Baker's Hill Road.

"Veronica?" Mrs. Shaw called fearfully. "Veronica, is that you?"

"Hi, Mom."

"Are you all right?" She pulled the children toward her, hugging them, half laughing, half crying. "You frightened the wits out of me."

"How did you find us?"

"As soon as I found your note I called Constable O'Toole and we went directly to the church. You weren't there and we were in the process of organizing a search party when we heard the gun shots."

The constable bent over the inert stranger. "Didn't expect to see this one again. He's out like a broken light." He turned to one of the villagers. "Better get the ambulance down here as quick as you can. Quite a nasty gash. What'd you hit him with?"

"Ah—" stammered Ben.

"With this." Veronica offered the dagger to her mother.

"So," said Marion Shaw, cradling the ancient blade in the palm of her hand, "there was a dagger after all. The British Museum will be pleased to have this beauty in its rightful place. Next you'll be telling us there really was a ghost named Jonathan Matthew."

Ben exchanged glances with Eddy and Veronica. "Wouldn't that be cool?"

The constable pushed his cap back. "We'll be putting this fellow away for a long time," he frowned.

Minutes later, with the stranger safely handcuffed and loaded into the ambulance, the villagers made their way back up to the high road. Thin strands of silver moonlight spread over the pond's still surface as Ben, Eddy and Veronica trekked back through the tall grass. When they finally turned to climb the hill, the clinging fog once again closed in over Sline's Oak Pond.

Epilogue

The dedication ceremony, due to begin at four o'clock, was still an hour away. But already the villagers had begun to arrive. They gathered in the churchyard, bathed in hazy shards of yellow sunlight, where they admired the newly restored north wall rising straight and strong above them.

The members of the Historical Society came next. So did the librarian and Mrs. Bell and the constable. Even old Mr. Woodson, who sat in a well-placed chair where he would be able to hear everything.

With heads barely apart, the villagers

whispered to one another. Back and forth they whispered and shook their heads about the incident at Sline's Oak Pond and about the children and the man who tried to steal the dagger.

And they whispered about Jonathan Matthew and the curse.

Only after the vicar had praised Marion Shaw's marvellous work and said a prayer of dedication did they begin to clap and laugh. Mrs. Shaw made a speech, and tea was served with small cookies and sandwiches and lots of raspberry squares.

Through it all, the children watched in silence from the stone fence beyond the graveyard. They watched until all the presentations were over and everyone had drifted, talking and laughing, back through the gatehouse arch.

They waited until the churchyard was empty and silent, until the slanting afternoon sun began to fail, until long grey shadows began creeping away from the edges of the gravestones and the church walls.

They watched because they knew he

would come. He wouldn't let them go back to Canada without telling them, somehow, that everything was all right now. So when the last of the light gave way to deep shadows, and wandering wisps of fog began to feel their way through the grass, the children were not surprised to see Jonathan Matthew slip silently among the gravestones, coming to rest, finally, beside the stone bench.

He stood as he had always stood, staring and pale, his rags hanging in tatters around his frail form, arms outstretched toward them. But this time he was not crying, and there was a strange, new light in his eyes.

"He's thanking us!" said Veronica. "I can feel it."

"Me too," responded Ben. "Look!"

And, to their amazement, the children saw the strange pale face of Jonathan Matthew lifted by a gentle little smile.

"Maybe he can rest now," Eddy suggested.

The figure remained for several long minutes before fading at last into the gloom of the churchyard.

"That's something I'll never forget!" breathed Eddy.

And, agreeing, the children made their way silently back to the high street, full of the peace of Jonathan Matthew—relieved for all time of the burden of King Richard's ancient curse.